HEATHER BOYD

USAT BESTSELLING AUTHOR

THE CHRISTMAS AFFAIR

REBEL HEARTS 3

Rebel Hearts Series

Book 1: The Wedding Affair
Book 2: An Affair of Honor
Book 3: The Christmas Affair
Book 4: An Affair so Right

THE CHRISTMAS AFFAIR
Copyright © 2016 by Heather Boyd
Edited by Anne Victory

AMY MELLISH MIGHT NEVER BE warm. She would freeze and no one would ever know her name. She would be just another homeless, unknown body they found during the spring thaw if she did not keep putting one foot ahead of the other.

She blew on her hands, encased in her late mother's best-but-worn gloves, and surveyed the bustling street ahead. Bond Street less than a week before Christmas was a busy time, though so cold this year. Few looked at her directly. No one moved out of her way.

It certainly was not the best time to lure a man to take their pleasure with her so she might afford a corner of a room in a drafty boardinghouse.

"A pox on the happily married," she muttered bitterly as a laughing couple almost barreled over her.

Amy had been overlooked all her life. As a child she had not had friends or family aside from her mother, and as an adult of two and twenty years, that was not likely to change. She was utterly alone, and as a result of her lack of proper protection in the form of chaperones, she was not innocent.

She was one of the impure, a fallen woman who relied on the wickedness of her customers to survive the harsh world of London's streets. It was not the life her mother had wanted for her, but it was the life she must live no matter how hard it seemed.

Unfortunately, she was not that successful in attracting interest in the middle of winter and had taken to the streets of London's busiest district in desperation for coin and customers.

She pushed on through the happy crowd, fretting over her desperate situation. She could do what one of the light-skirts on the last street corner had just done—made a show of unbuttoning her threadbare coat and flashed her breasts to a passing gentleman. The portly fellow had ogled her but had not flicked out a coin. He had smiled and then moved on with his own business. The woman had taken the loss of custom with good spirits and hurried to cover herself again. Amy considered her very brave. Undressing, even partially, while the snow fell, and the winds howled, was not pleasant. While she silently applauded the woman's tenacity and fortitude under trying circumstances, Amy was not willing to surrender any more of her body heat to the uncertainty of fickle male whim.

She had to be practical and thrifty with her favors.

"Watch where you're going!"

Amy jerked up her chin and met the hard stare of a well-heeled heavy-set gent of middle years. On his arm was an expensively dressed woman who positively sneered at Amy's presence on their path. Amy shuffled aside, feet sinking into a deep patch of snow that reached above the top of her ankle-high boots. The couple took their time passing, and Amy was shivering in earnest once more when she could proceed.

She stamped her feet after they were gone and shook the snow from the hem of her heavy garments.

"People are always in too much of a hurry," a contemptuous male voice remarked nearby.

She turned around for the source of the voice and found a fellow standing just inside an alley in the shadows, smoking from a weathered pipe. He seemed of middle age or perhaps older, but it was hard to tell with his cap pulled low over his eyes.

Amy smothered her disappointment. She preferred a younger customer. They were a little more giving of their coin and often cleaner, but she would make do with whatever she got. "Some are indeed."

He moved to the edge of the shadows but did not step out into the street to meet her. His eyes beneath the cap were fierce and his expression sour. "Most don't see the beauty they cast aside. Not me though. I've got my eyes wide open. I see you."

"How kind," Amy said calmly enough, but her skin prickled with a warning.

From time to time, Amy had met men whose interest in her brought unpleasant sensations. She did not feel at all safe near this fellow. Despite his neat outward appearance, there was something about his demeanor that warned her to keep a distance. He could be dangerous.

His clothes were good quality, but it was what lay beneath that made a difference. Even the best-dressed men could hurt a whore. She had heard enough, witnessed enough firsthand, to heed her own instincts. She nodded to him, intending to move along.

He jerked his head toward the alley behind him. "Why don't you come over here and we can warm each other for a bit?"

She pretended to be shocked. "Sir!"

His expression grew menacing in an instant. "Think you're too good for the likes of me? I know what you are."

Amy needed coin desperately, but not so desperately as to risk misadventure with someone as changeable as him. "I am a lady, sir, and what you suggest is indecent. Leave me be or I shall call the watch."

She spun around, but not before she heard the sound of a soft moan come from the dark alley behind the fellow. Amy hurried on, crossing the street to the bakery side, and slipping in behind a chattering group. She took a moment to catch her breath, stealing the warmth from the ovens deep into her lungs for as long as she dared. And then when an older woman swept past carrying a heaped basket, she followed her out onto the street again.

A quick glance around confirmed the dangerous fellow had not followed her to the bakery.

The woman with the basket turned to her. "Can I help you, dearie?" She had the face of kindness, but her eyes were shrewd as she took in Amy's threadbare coat.

"No, but thank you."

The older woman hesitated. "You're very pale."

"The cold," Amy murmured, but then that moan she had overheard from the alley came to mind. "A conversation with a stranger a short time ago has overset my nerves. It's nothing, I'm sure."

"Oh, what did he say?" The woman adjusted her basket, waiting for a juicy bit of gossip.

"Nothing untoward, thankfully, but as I was walking away, I swear I heard a moan come from the alley behind him."

The woman's eyes widened. "Not again."

The woman spun back for the bakery, shouting a man's name, and disappeared with her basket of baked goods.

Amy sighed, lamenting the fact that the memory of the smell of freshly baked bread was going to torture her all day and likely all night.

Unfortunately, Amy had no choice but to push on in search of a customer. A shy smile, a flutter of lashes, were all she had to bring a gentleman into her arms in the right circumstances. In the biting cold of the afternoon, however, she was not having much luck, and she needed funds to escape the aching cold of winter that was sure to envelop the city tonight.

Another couple passed her, laughing as they went. "A pox on all happy couples," she said aloud and then prayed she had not been overheard.

She had best keep her thoughts to herself, or she would never appeal to anyone. Aside from the dangerous fellow, she usually had good luck in the shopping district, though her usual haunts had attracted a rougher crowd of late. Amy had no wish to be passed around a group of men for the fee of a single client. As long as she was not overly brazen about what she was there for, she had found she was left largely to her own devices in the proper neighborhoods.

And it was usually so much cleaner, safer, nicer all round in this part of town. She lifted her thoughts to the path ahead and arranged her face into a pleasing expression.

There were certain shops, however, that she did not like to linger near for long, and they were just ahead. The pastry shop always made her empty stomach complain, and the fine merchandise displayed in the Cabot's Haberdashery windows made her yearn for the past and the coin she did not possess.

The dream of one day having funds to buy whatever she liked gave her something to hope for though. If her circumstances changed and she had funds at the ready to spoil herself with, she might yet be a regular customer at either establishment.

However, she would not be able to frequent either if one of the proprietors—both very proper gents and handsome—discovered how she earned her living.

CHAPTER TWO

MR. HARPER CABOT OF CABOT'S Haberdashery, London, surveyed the new stock and his domain with approval. Trade that day had been brisk and satisfyingly lucrative, the delayed shipment he had received at midday had eased his cares. Profits should be up this month despite the biting cold, and the new man he had employed last month had borne the brunt of the heavy lifting without complaint.

Mr. Robin Pelaw was working out perfectly and handling his demanding clientele with the utmost respect. His youth and handsomeness proved a gentle lure for women who frequented the busy Bond Street shopping district. Harper had a knack of knowing what people most wanted. Pelaw's glib tongue and easy manner was genuine enough to ensure he sold to most of his customers on the same day.

The new man did a much better job of being pleasing than he or his other longtime employee, Godfrey Hunter, had done of late.

"Is there anything else you need done tonight, Mr. Cabot?" Mr. Pelaw asked as he placed the final bolts of new fabric on display for the regular customers. The more costly fabrics were already locked away in a private room at the rear of the shop, only available for inspection by those with the funds to pay for any damage their eager pawing might inflict.

"You can remove the crates we stacked out back first thing tomorrow, but the buttons have become jumbled again. They'll need to be sorted before you go home," he said, casting a rueful glance toward the always-popular table display. He was very glad to pass on a task that had become a daily bother since his wife had passed away. Diana Cabot, his late wife, had enjoyed sorting the many colors, sizes, and shapes at the end of each long workday while he tallied the books.

He missed her still.

Pelaw groaned and moved to the table covered in tiny jars. "Yes, sir."

"Stop thinking of her," Hunter said from a safe distance, his voice subdued.

"I cannot help the way I feel." He folded the lace bolt carefully and set it aside. "Everything here reminds me of her."

Hunter set his scissors safely away into the workbench drawer. "You need a new woman to turn your mind."

Harper clenched his jaw. "A temporary solution to a permanent affliction at best."

Hunter drew close, folding his apron. "She was only one woman in a hundred pretty faces that have passed through your front door."

"She was my world, Hunter."

"No, your shop was your world, and you feel guilty she died alone. That's the real reason you're so bloody unhappy and doing your best to make us feel the same."

He pressed his lips together. He couldn't deny the charge.

Hunter bid him good night then and went on his way, a bachelor in search of amusement, and thankfully, this time he did not try to drag Harper along.

Harper preferred to wallow in his memories of happier times. He'd had a vastly satisfying married life. He had met Diana, the eldest daughter of the nearby baker one summer afternoon. She had been just nineteen, late coming out due to a death in the family, and they had struck the right note immediately. A month later he'd asked for her hand in marriage, and they'd had ten years of happiness in this shop together before influenza had robbed her of her health and then her life.

He missed her presence at his side—her wise words of advice and quiet strength supporting him in his endeavors. He was indeed guilty of neglect too. The day she had died, she had died alone, upstairs in their apartment on Christmas morning. He had left her side, thinking it was for but a moment, to attend an important client who had arrived unexpectedly. When he had returned upstairs, flush with the success of a lucrative transaction, she had already slipped away.

Since burying Diana, every day had become an effort to rise from his empty bed and get on with his lonely life. A routine had been his salvation. Once he was among the bolts of fabrics and customer demands, he could forget that his life was so very empty in every other respect save professional achievement.

As the clock struck four o'clock, Harper moved to the front door and pulled down the shade on the white world outside. Snow had been falling steadily since daybreak, muting the sounds of the world beyond his shop. It was too cold to venture out to his club or to visit a married friend's happy home for the pleasure of their conversation and excellent food. He would stay in yet again and ignore the empty space beside him for another endless night.

"Good night, Mr. Cabot."

"Good evening, Pelaw," he said before throwing the bolts on the door to protect his property.

Closing up had once been his late wife's job, and he was reminded how different his life had become just by completing the simple task. Cabot's Haberdashery had once boasted *& Son* behind his surname. Since his wife had not conceived by the time his father had died, he had put those hopes aside. Despite Hunter's claim that women were replaceable, he found it hard to consider remarriage or even to contemplate courting another woman. Diana would be impossible to replace anyway. She had devoted more of her life to the business as each year passed and her arms remained empty of a child for her to love. She had rarely shown her disappointment to others, but he was aware of her private pain.

They had talked it over, had each hoped for a miracle, but it had not helped. They had remained childless, and Harper had set his ambitions for the future and the longevity of his business aside.

He drew the blinds down over the south window and then straightened the ladies' hat display. His wife had loved hats of all styles and features. Thanks to her fine taste, and her subtle improvement of his, his customers now never lacked pretty things to wear upon their heads.

It had been a year since her passing, and he missed having someone to go home to, someone to lavish his attention on and spoil.

Not that home was far. He had lived above his place of business for a dozen years now and found the arrangement imminently convenient to the long hours he kept.

As he reached for the north window blind, he spotted a woman staring at a fur muffler displayed on a bed of pink silk wraps. Thinking she might be one last customer for the day, he paused before she noticed him to give her time to make her mind up about coming inside.

The woman's bright green eyes gleamed as she beheld his wares. He was used to that look in female customers when it came to his many items, and he tried to anticipate what she might fancy. Her slender fingers rose to caress the glass between her and the object of her interest. It was then he noticed the hole in her glove. Was she interested in replacing her damaged pair tonight or just looking for what she might come back for another day?

He studied her more closely, noting the thin scarf wrapped high about her neck, the soft but dated felt cap perched over dark, inky locks. He could not discern her age, and for him that was a rare occurrence. He could usually decide a woman's maturity, and likely interest in accessories, within a few moments of seeing her.

He eased deeper into the shadows and continued his observations unobserved, trying to figure her out.

Her shapely red lips expelled warm air into the chill of London in a short puff. A strange feeling swelled inside him when her pink tongue darted out to lick those lips.

He felt the stirrings of desire, which in itself was unusual for him with any prospective customer.

She shivered noticeably as a gust of wind stirred up the snow around her until she was almost lost from view. Her pert nose was red from the cold and wrinkled in dissatisfaction as her attention moved to another item on display.

He could reopen the shop for a few moments should she merely be waiting for her friends to join her. He glanced behind her to see where her companions might be, or a waiting carriage, and saw only the empty pavement and street behind. She should return to her carriage before she froze to death.

But there was no stopped carriage on the street.

She was alone, which was odd for this hour of the evening.

A single woman could be subjected to the worst sort of behavior by any number of scoundrels on Bond Street after dark.

A pair of well-dressed fellows strolled past, and he held his breath as she glanced their way. Although a woman alone would do well to avoid the attention of strangers, she lifted her chin and smiled warmly at them. Were they friends of hers?

One of the fellows nudged his companion, a knowing smile brightening his features, and the pair came closer to the woman. Harper reached for the door handle, prepared to intervene. After a moment or two of conversation, the pair moved on. The woman's face fell.

Harper cursed. She was not a prospective customer, just a poor woman attracted by the pretty things in his windows on her way to somewhere else. More than likely, she was one of London's light-skirts in search of a gentleman to offer up his warm bed on this coldest of nights. And there he was staring at her as if she were a proper lady in need of his protection.

Harper reached for the blind and drew it down over the display, utterly disappointed that the first time he had experienced stirrings of arousal had been for a completely unsuitable woman.

CHAPTER THREE

AMY STOOD BACK to admire her handiwork in the dim light, rather proud of her only stroke of good fortune that day. The tiny collection of empty crates she'd found tossed behind Cabot's Haberdashery would provide a better night's sleep than anything she could think of given her lack of funds and location. Because of the cold, or perhaps the approaching holiday, she had failed to tempt any gentleman that day or night and was entirely without funds. Even the whores were scarce on the street corners, which meant they'd had all the luck while Amy had none.

Without coin to pay for a rented room, she had no other option but to make do with a night outside in the elements and be grateful for the meager shelter. Unfortunately, she could not shake her fear that the dangerous fellow she had met earlier would find her. Amy tested the weight of the two sticks of wood she had found at the entrance to the lane and wondered what harm they might do if she had to use them against an attacker. Poor protection indeed, but it was all she had at hand.

As usual, her best defense would be to run for safety, but no close safe haven sprang readily to mind.

After a quick glance left and right, Amy wormed her way into the pile and huddled in as comfortable a position as she was able, blowing on her cold fingertips, which she couldn't see in the utter dark of her secluded hideaway. She kept her weapons at her side, within easy reach. It would not be the worst night she'd ever spent alone since her mother's death a year ago, but this makeshift home was better than freezing to death in the frigid wind that had sprung up in the past hour.

Hopefully, it would not all fall down on her head in the middle of the night and break her skull. And maybe the dangerous man had forgotten his interest in her, too.

She pulled her mother's scarf up over her tender, chilled nose and cheeks and let her breath warm her skin, lamenting her pale complexion. She had caught her reflection in the Cabot's window display and had almost cried over the red hue of her nose and cheeks. No doubt the ruddiness of her features had not added to her appeal that night, and there was not much she could do about it so late in the evening. Crying over her ill luck would only make her redden further.

She was much more appealing in summer when her skin caught a touch of color from the sunshine, but warmth and fair days were half a year away. Tomorrow she would take greater pains to protect herself from the wind and the uncomfortable flush a winter season had brought to her skin, and hope to turn a nice gentleman's head instead of the nasty talking pair she'd just met.

Gentleman was a term that was hardly applicable to those crude scoundrels, and she'd learned to apply it sparingly to the male gender.

She hummed a little Christmas tune that her mother had sung often while she'd baked Christmas treats in the home she'd grown up in on the outskirts of London and then clamped her lips shut as her eyes stung with fresh tears. She blinked, shaking the moisture away before her lashes grew too damp. The festive season brought so many memories that, for a little while, she could almost forget that her life was unbearable. Of course, reality always returned to cut to the bone and remind her how desperate her situation had become.

How many more months, weeks, days could she live like this? Her belly ached in a constant reminder that starvation was never far away.

Amy hugged her knees, trying to fixate on something pleasant to warm her thoughts away from bitterness.

Her mother would have loved the Cabot's window display this year. The man, Cabot, had a gift for arranging his goods with such an eye to a woman's desires that it became so very hard to look away. If only she had the coin for a fur muffler, her hands might never be cold again.

It was also very hard to look away from the very handsome Mr. Cabot when he occasionally stepped out of his shop. He had never noticed her passing him, few did, but there was something so very arresting about the shopkeeper's face that made her insides tumble over.

It was not fear of him or even shame that she passed unnoticed. She thought perhaps she felt lust for him, which in her line of work was an utterly ridiculous emotion to feel for any man.

Yet she made sure to pass by Mr. Cabot's bright shop every week just to see if the feelings he stirred had passed. They still had not as of today. Longing for the unattainable man to notice her was a foolish occupation since he was already happily married, but her consideration of his appeal and form kept her mind occupied when her body was entertaining other men.

She shifted a little, disgruntled with her train of thought, and bumped the crate to her left but not enough to move it far. How foolish to think of a married man. Amy had caught a glimpse of

Mrs. Cabot a few times. She was lovely and very attractive in her elegant clothes. So very, very good.

A boot scraped over cobblestone nearby. "Who's there?"

Amy turned her face toward the voice, trembling at the gruff male barking out orders beyond her meager shelter. Had the dangerous man found her or was it the watch?

She made herself very small and hoped that whoever it was might go away. If she was quiet, they might think they had merely heard a rat scampering about the refuse. The boots came closer until she could see a shape through the gaps in her construction. She did not believe she could be seen, but she covered her mouth to quiet her breathing. If she was overlooked and the man went on his way, she might stay undetected until morning when she crept out. She hoped so.

"Show yourself, or I'll call the watch," the man demanded.

Amy breathed a sigh of relief. The dangerous man was not the sort to have threatened her with the watch. He would avoid authority as much as she would, perhaps more.

It must be someone else entirely who had discovered her. Still, she could not have that sort of trouble. A night in a cell was bound to end up with her taken advantage of by any number of unsavory characters. Best come forward now so she would be left alone.

"Please don't call the watch," she begged.

Amy grasped her weapons and crawled out of her makeshift home on hands and knees then stood swiftly, holding her hands clenched at her sides. She faced the stranger, heart leaping out of her chest in relief the next moment. It was the nice man from the haberdashery—Mr. Cabot himself.

Amy quickly dropped her unnecessary weapons before he noticed and made an effort to shake out her coat. She had to brazen this out so Mr. Cabot would not send her on her way.

"Good evening, Mr. Cabot." She dipped a curtsy, deciding

that even a fallen woman should mind her manners this close to Christmas. "Happy Christmas."

He blinked at her greeting, then scowled at her makeshift home. "What are you doing there?"

"Nothing." She ran a quick hand over her frayed coat and smiled warmly. Surely Mr. Cabot would not mind her encampment behind his shop too much if she were very quiet and unobtrusive. "It's a lovely night for a stroll, but shouldn't you get back inside to the warmth? Your wife will be wondering where you are."

He stared at her a long moment and then blinked. "My wife passed away."

A hard lump formed in her throat, and she took a step toward him. So that explained why she'd not seen his wife recently. But then, to her shame, she had only ever really cared about the ever-changing window display and Mr. Cabot's fine and unavailable presence. "I am so sorry."

He nodded sharply, his lips pressing together, and glanced aside. He crossed his arms over his chest. "It was sudden."

Amy took another step closer as he shivered. He was not dressed to be out of doors. His hair was wet and slicked back from his face, and he wore a banyan of thick and luxurious brocade, the type a wealthy lord might wear in the privacy of his own bedchamber.

He looked as if he had been getting ready for bed.

A *warm* bed.

An *empty* bed.

It took a second to formulate a new plan for her night, but then she felt shame and disgust in herself. She could not attempt to seduce a man who was grieving. It was not fair to him and would only lead to her own humiliation. She had had enough of that for one day. "You should go in, sir."

He refocused his attention on her as the wind spun snow around them in a white mist. "Were you going to sleep under those boxes tonight?"

She hesitated to answer but then nodded. What was the point of lying about it? Since her mother's death, she had learned to accept that she did not deserve anything more than to be where she was. Being fatherless, and now a whore, ensured she was scorned wherever she went. "I will be quiet. I promise. You won't even know I'm outside your door."

"Have you no home, no one to wonder where you are?"

He frowned when she shook her head again and then glanced around at the deserted, dirty lane.

He really needed to return indoors before his hair froze. Amy backed away. If she pretended to leave, he would not have an excuse to linger. Once he had gone inside, she could sneak back and quietly creep into her shelter again.

"Please go back inside before you catch a chill. I will go. I don't want to be any trouble."

He stared at her so long she started to tremble for an entirely different reason. Mr. Cabot saw her at last, but this was not how she had imagined the moment. She had nothing to recommend herself. No money to spend in his shop, no beauty with which to capture his attention.

He followed her a few steps and then bent down to pick up the sticks she'd dropped when he'd first made himself known to her.

He turned them over in his bare hands a moment, eyes widening, but then shook his head repeatedly. He flung them aside and gestured to his open rear door. "You should come in. There's a safer and warmer place for you with me."

CHAPTER FOUR

HARPER CLOSED and locked the door behind the young woman, a little bewildered by his actions. He was asking for trouble by bringing a stranger into his home and place of business. What did he want with the woman?

To prevent her from freezing to death outside his door was certainly a possibility. He could have called the watch to move her on but could not bring himself to give her trouble of that sort. He could have walked away and gone to his bed alone and never thought of her ever again.

Yet once he had discovered the source of the noise was a woman, and a pretty one too, with nothing but two sticks of firewood to defend herself with, his hesitation had vanished. She was in need of his kindness and protection, so he had invited her in.

He ignored the little voice in the back of his mind that suggested he indulge in wickedness with her if she was willing once she was warm. If she was indeed the sort of woman he suspected she might be.

He shuffled his feet, uncertain how to proceed. "You seem to know me, but I am ashamed to say I don't recall your name."

"Miss Amy Mellish of Brentwood, Mr. Cabot." She smiled, and his heart did a strange little flip at the earnestness of her expression. "I'm not surprised I seem a stranger."

"You're a long way from home." Perhaps she was not a street-walker. "Refresh my memory please."

"My mother brought me to London when I was a girl, and she purchased a yard of German lace from your late father for a gown she was to make for a customer. You were there, but we never spoke as much as one word to each other. It was my first time in London, and I was quite overwhelmed by the sights and sounds around me." She sighed a little wistfully. "Your family still has the nicest shop windows in all of Bond Street. I walk past your windows quite often on my... errands."

"Thank you." He was a little astonished by the compliment. "I apologize for not remembering you straightaway."

"That's quite all right, sir. You have a great many customers, and I'm sure you cannot remember them all." She looked around, a quick peek at her surroundings, then stared at his face. "You should dry your hair before you take a chill."

He self-consciously raised his hand, discovering his damp hair was almost crisp. "I had forgotten. Please, won't you come into the kitchen? There's a fire burning."

At the mention of fire, Amy shot in the direction he indicated. The kitchen, a place that had not seen much use since his wife's death, was large and toasty warm.

Amy skirted the copper tub, still filled from his weekly bath, and held her hands to the range. She moaned, and his heart flipped again at the earthy, eager sound she made.

"You must be frozen."

"Not so much as last winter." She used her teeth to remove her gloves and rubbed her hands briskly. "The days have been very mild."

"But not the nights," he countered. Drawing closer to her, he tried to judge her age, which proved frustrating. His father had died five years ago. She stood only as high as his chin, and her tiny stature made her appear somewhat frail and very young.

Miss Mellish glanced around. "Is anyone else here? A servant?"

"No, and I don't keep a live-in. I have a woman come in to clean once a week. That is all the help I need these days."

He was babbling, and he bit his tongue to stop the flow.

"I'm sure you have the right of it," she agreed.

He moved past her and added more coal to the fire. Miss Mellish eased a little closer to the hearth until she brushed against his side. He caught her chilled hands as she stretched them toward the open flames.

"Be careful you don't burn yourself."

She allowed him to hold her hands still a moment before stroking his with her thumb. "I will."

Her touch was hesitant but inflamed his soul to an alarming degree. He wanted her to keep touching him, more than he ever imagined he could want of any stranger.

When he stood back, she took his place before the hearth but kept to a safer distance. Harper moved to the other side of the fire and perched on a low stool, worried that his needy thoughts might be obvious to her.

He grasped a length of thick linen and rubbed his hair with it to absorb the remaining moisture.

They sat in companionable silence, listening to the faint hiss of burning coal while they both warmed themselves again.

It was an odd moment for him. He had never before invited a stranger into his private quarters, and he was not properly dressed to receive visitors. Miss Mellish did not appear at all disturbed by this lack of proper clothing. In fact, she seemed rather at ease.

He glanced at the copper tub, still full of warm water. He had yet to discard it after his bath. That was what he had been about to do before he heard singing outside his door and then a bump that had prompted him to investigate properly.

It might be a waste to discard water so obviously clean, but with no one living with him now, he had no choice but to toss it outside. However, perhaps Miss Mellish might long for a bath to warm her through and through? She seemed fresh enough to his eye, but according to his late wife, a woman's attitude toward her body odors was entirely different from a man's.

He cleared his throat and gestured to the tub. "I usually bathe on Friday's and am about to toss out the water, but perhaps, I wonder if you might care for..."

Miss Mellish's eyes rounded. "A bath? Truly?"

He nodded slowly, astonished by the excitement in her eyes. "If you would like, I can reheat some of the water."

"Oh, thank you. You are so kind." She smiled shyly. "I would like to soak above almost anything."

He refilled two pails from the bath water and set them on the range to heat again. He thought that would be sufficient for her needs. Amy stood, eyeing the bath and the slowly warming pails of water. He could see her impatience in the way she wrung her hands, and it made him feel very good that he had voiced his idea.

When the water was ready and returned to the copper tub, he stepped back. "I will leave you to enjoy it."

She bit her lip as she stripped her coat away, revealing a serviceable but plain blue gown beneath. She paused with her fingers on the buttons of the bodice and then undid the first one. "You don't have to go."

She continued to unbutton her front-opening gown and quickly tugged on the cord of her chemise, exposing the tops of her breasts. Fierce arousal gripped him as she wriggled her hips to slide the material down her legs. As her slender body came into view, he grew light-headed from lust. Her skin was flawlessly pale, her nipples a delicate pink. It seemed an age since he had touched such a pert pair as Miss Mellish possessed, and for a moment he could not move or breathe.

But he did move eventually; he averted his eyes and backed to the door before he embarrassed himself. "Enjoy your bath."

Once outside, he allowed the door to close slowly on the enticing view.

He wanted her, and he did not quite trust himself.

Behind the door Miss Mellish sighed so deeply he felt her disappointment in him all the way through the heavy wood. He almost laughed, but then she moaned and splashed around in his copper tub for at least ten minutes. Listening to her bathe was fascinating and frustrating, though he would not curb her enjoyment for the world. He smiled at the noises she made and leaned against the wall to enjoy the moments of pure indulgence. It had been so long since he'd had a woman under his roof that his heart could not help but lift at the sound of her pleasure. He had someone to look after again, and his gray world had brightened immeasurably.

He turned, inspired by an idea to make the most of his good luck. If she had been disappointed in his going away, he would make her happy for his return. He strode for the ready-made lady's apparel and hunted through the assortment of delicate garments. When he had what he wanted—a heavy robe, nightgown, thick gloves, and a pair of stockings and garters—he tossed them over his arm and strode back to the kitchen.

He took a breath to calm himself and tapped on the door. "May I come in?"

Water splashed. "Of course, Mr. Cabot."

He stepped inside, ready to make a discreet and speedy delivery, but stopped dead. Her long hair was darkly wet against her pale chest and curved around her splendid breasts, the tips of which were suspended in the soapy water. Miss Mellish was partially immersed in the tub, but the way her limbs were arranged left him in no doubt she was a woman who would welcome his advances. He had never seen anything more openly erotic in all his years. He could have her tonight and let go of the past. Make love to her with no emotional commitments.

For a fee, he reminded himself roundly. A woman of her nature was always after coin. The question was always how much he would have to pay for such a distraction from loneliness.

He laid the garments over a chair. "I thought you might like to slip these on after your bath."

She pulled her knees up to her chest and wrapped her arms around them. "You are very kind, but you shouldn't trouble yourself too much on my account."

"It's no bother." He eyed the bath. "Is the water growing cold?"

"It is perfect still, but I'm ready to get out." She set her hands to the sides of the tub and rose, her gaze holding his. Harper was not able to keep his eyes off her body for long. Water droplets skidded down her limbs like lovers and revealed a slender body he longed to touch. She stepped out on the fireplace side and brought a length of towel to her face.

He stood immobile as she wiped water from her arms and torso. The delicate twisting of her body before the hearth made him hard as stone. He was astounded by the degree of wild lust he felt for this stranger. No doubt the year of abstinence after Diana's sickness had taken its toll on his libido. He felt fevered.

He stepped closer to Amy. "May I offer assistance?"

The glance she directed at him over her shoulder made his heart skip a beat. She was astonished, but the expression soon turned to delight. "If you wish. You may do anything you like as thanks for letting me luxuriate in that bath."

He took the towel and gently patted the water droplets lingering on her shoulder, then meandered toward her spine. As he continued downward to her pert little bottom, stroking over her skin gently, a little moan escaped her lips.

Miss Mellish was either a very good actress or entirely sincere in her appreciation of his attention. He chose to believe the latter and gathered her hair to squeeze it between the ends of the towel. Such long hair would take an age to dry, so he slung it over her shoulder, across her breasts, and returned to drying her body.

When her skin was without even one droplet of water, he turned her back to the hearth. She had such long dark hair, and he flicked it over her shoulder, listening to the water hiss as it struck the range. He teased his fingers into the wet locks, shaking water from them and finding snarls.

"Lean against me," he murmured. "This could take a while."

"It always does. I thought perhaps I must cut it off soon. It is difficult to dress easily without someone to help, and if I sell it to a wigmaker, I should make a few shillings, don't you think?"

"Don't you dare cut it," he protested, thoroughly enjoying the slide of her dark hair through his fingers as it dried. "Beautiful hair such as this must be protected and kept on the head of the person who grew it."

"If you insist, I will for now." The little woman pressed her head against his chest and sighed, her warm breath penetrating his light shirt. "You are so warm, sir," she said, burrowing closer.

He groaned as his cock jerked. It was lust, pure and simple. His body was on fire with a naked woman in his arms.

Her fingers roamed his back and sides timidly as he threaded his through her long dark strands, aiding the drying. He gently worked out the knots and snarls, and twenty minutes or so later, her hair was straight and shining in the candlelight.

He gathered her hair together and then let it fall.

She shivered. "Thank you."

He took up the robe and slid her arms into the sleeves. It was a little large but covered her sufficiently to keep the chill at bay for now. "Stockings next."

Harper caught her about the waist and plunked her on the table. "May I ask a question?"

"Certainly, sir."

He took the stool and sat before her. "How long have you been like this? Alone. Living without protection."

"It's a year since my mother died." She set both feet on his lap and allowed him to encase her leg in the thick white stocking. "I had a nice position for a while as a maid, but I couldn't stay."

"Why couldn't you?" He grunted as her wiggling toes drew dangerously close to his groin, then selected a rose-pink garter, and tied it under her knee.

"The master of the house liked the maids too much." She sighed. "His wife always blamed them for his indiscretions and slapped them around the face afterward. It was only a matter of time before he turned his attention in my direction. I did not encourage him or like her very much. I certainly wasn't going to allow her to strike me for her husband's lecherous inclinations."

Harper gritted his teeth. "My wife passed a year ago." He caressed her leg. "I've never done this before—brought a woman who was not my wife into my home. Not when I was married and not since I've been widowed."

Miss Mellish brushed his hair back from his eyes. "You were a better husband than most, I expect."

His hands trembled tying the last ribbon in place. If she knew the way his mind worked at the moment, she wouldn't keep thinking that of him. He was feeling decidedly lecherous, but he fought his lust. "Why is there no one looking after you? Why are you this way?"

"When my mother died, I was on my own. No dowry, no benefactor. I had no choice unless I wished to starve. I had to work at something." She sighed again. "And I had already been ruined, so it was inevitable I come to London to earn my way in the world."

He glanced up. "I'm sorry."

"Don't be." She touched his head again. "You were not the one who forced me to this life."

He swallowed a hard lump in his throat. "You're not even angry."

"I was indeed very angry at the time." Her nails scraped his skull, and he shuddered as she teased the curve of his ear. "However, a lot has changed in a year. I might have needed to compromise my principals to a fair degree, but no one owns me. I have learned that circumstances require a more practical mindset be exercised when you only possess one asset. I have something I think you want, Mr. Cabot. I'm willing to be very thorough in pleasing you."

She was so brave.

"Is that so?"

"Oh, yes." Her toes wiggled in his lap, stroking up his length softly and back down with a little more force. "I know you want me, sir. The question is *how*."

CHAPTER FIVE

HARPER HAD NEVER REALLY DISCUSSED the form of taking his pleasure before it was happening. To do so seemed a decidedly cold arrangement, but he supposed with a prostitute there were always necessary negotiations. "What do you offer?"

She smiled and leaned down. Her hand dangled where her restless foot had recently teased, and she brushed across the bulge in his trousers with her delicate fingers. Her robe had parted and revealed her pert little breasts. He grew very hot thinking of pressing his cheek against one, taking the peak into his mouth, and feasting upon it.

A wicked smile curved her lips. "I can use my hand to bring you to completion. Or my mouth," she whispered as she rested her cheek against his. Her breath against the shell of his ear made him quake.

He caught her face and pressed her to his cheek. "Tempting."

"Or I could lie back on this very sturdy-looking table and let you have your wicked way with me." She drew back and met his gaze, her eyes bright with her own arousal. She licked her lips seductively and then held her bottom lip between her teeth a moment. "Or all three."

He'd known what he wanted from the moment he had laid eyes on Amy standing at his window. He just wanted her. Intimately. Completely. He wanted hours of pleasure to banish his loneliness. "And the fee for a whole night?"

She appeared surprised and glanced down. "I've never spent a whole night with a customer before."

He lowered his face, hiding his satisfaction that what they did together would be a unique experience for her. "The most sought-after courtesans are said to be worth the price of financial ruin."

"I am not greedy, sir."

A shiver raced over his body at the meek way she said *sir*. He liked that. "Your body, your hand, and perhaps your mouth," he whispered. "Twice over."

She fisted her hand in his shirt. "Whatever do you think the experience would be worth, sir."

He named so generous enough a sum that her eyes widened. She nodded as Harper cupped her cheek and brushed his thumb across her flaming skin to reassure her he was in earnest. Despite their negotiations, she was surprisingly shy about the business of the fee.

"Then lie back."

Miss Mellish did so slowly as he stood over her. The robe had parted, revealing delicate pink skin fresh from her bath with goose-flesh racing over her. Her nipples were puckered to points, but he was not entirely certain if it was arousal or from the cold. He would rather her aroused than cold, so he tugged one side over her exposed breast and kept the other free for exploration.

As he had learned from drying her, Amy's skin was soft under his fingertips. He brushed the side of her breast and then covered it with his whole hand. Against his palm, her nipple was a hard point. He rubbed her lightly with the flat of his hand as her breath caught, then dragged his hand down before bending to kiss her nipple. He took the peak into his mouth, lapping, and tracing around the tip until she squirmed. He suckled harder, pulling her body up from the table so her back arched into him.

Touching her was heaven.

He switched sides, making sure that his lover had no chance of becoming chilled.

He closed his eyes as instinct, and her tiny gasps of pleasure, guided him to discover what pleased her best. Her fingers were in his hair, nails scratching his skull as she gasped and moaned beneath his attention.

When he had taken his fill of her breasts, he moved to kiss her trembling stomach, lingering on her soft belly before lightly kissing the nest of dark curls protecting her quim. Amy shifted, and he carefully secured her robe more tightly about her chest. "I don't want you to take a chill, but this might take a while," he whispered, pulling a stool up to the table. "I want to taste you."

As he went to lower his head, Amy scrambled backward on the table, drawing her knees together.

She clutched the robe over her chest, eyes wide. "What are you doing?"

"Kissing you." His eyes widened in shock. "Have you never had a man put his mouth on your sex before?"

She shook her head very quickly.

"It is very pleasant. If done well, it is said to be better than intercourse for a woman."

Her brow furrowed. "That isn't necessary."

"It is for me. I'm making love to you and not just for my own pleasure." He thought a moment. "I would pay double for the privilege of licking you there with my tongue."

Her eyelashes fluttered and her breath came a little faster. "Why?"

"Because it will excite you." He met her gaze, keen to convince her. If she was not aroused enough, she might not enjoy his being inside her, and he had to be inside her soon. "Trust me on this. If you dislike the sensations, I will stop."

She nodded and relaxed a little, but he could see her doubts had not been banished. He would have to prove he knew a woman's body better than those selfish swains who had not given her needs a second thought before.

He stroked her trembling thighs and lightly kissed them. When he returned to her quim, he used his hand first, so she was better prepared for the sensation of being touched there. However, he quickly pressed his mouth to her folds and acquainted himself with the woman's taste while she grew used to having his head buried between her legs. He lapped at her lower lips gently but persistently until she moaned at last. He raised his head and met her gaze.

Her tentative smile was a relief. "Are you done?"

"Not even a little." Harper shoved her legs farther apart and ate at her greedily. The taste of a woman was the best part of being a man. To control a woman's passions so thoroughly she became desperate for completion was his goal. Amy was utterly delicious, and soon her weak protests turned to loud pleas for more. She squirmed and moaned to everything he did, so brokenly that he concluded she had never expected the slightest bit of excitement in all the times she had been taken.

He stabbed his tongue inside her a few times and then returned to teasing her clitoris. Amy made a choking noise, and her fingers fluttered over his head. He caught her hand, tucked it under her bottom, and held it there firmly, using it as an anchor to keep her exactly where he wanted her.

She moaned deeply as he lapped and curled his tongue around the hard bud of her arousal. When he sucked again, her hips bucked, and she shuddered against him, gasping his name. She fell apart with a startled cry of indescribable surprise.

He eased back a little, beyond satisfied by her response, and grinned.

He moved to his feet and stared into her face until she opened her eyes. Amy appeared quite dazed, and he waited a moment for her shock to subside before he freed his cock. He stroked himself a few times, waiting for her to come back to him.

She eased up on one elbow, her other hand reaching to touch. She could only tease the head because he kept himself out of reach. "Sir?"

"Relax again. Show me your breasts."

A little smile twisted her lips as she jerked open her robe and revealed her breasts and hard, pointed nipples. He set one hand on her hip, the head of his cock at her entrance, and teased himself with her moisture. When his cock head was thoroughly damp, wet from her arousal, he pushed into her very slowly, watching her face the entire time for any sign of distress. He did not really know her and what she might prefer, so he set a slow and gentle claiming until he was sure of her comfort.

But being inside her was heaven.

He had missed these moments of possession with Diana, of knowing he was part of something greater than himself. Amy swallowed and then she reached to grasp his arms.

Harper caught one hand and brought her fingers to his lips. He kissed her knuckles as he sank deep. When he released her hand, he braced himself against the tabletop at both sides of her head, caging her beneath him. "Is that all right, Miss Mellish?"

"Indeed, it is, Mr. Cabot." She smiled shyly. "You feel very good inside me."

The compliment went to both his heads. Gentleness went out the window as he began to thrust with more force. Amy arched her back as he battered her body with his desire, drawing out the moment for as long as possible. When he was ready to spill his seed, he jerked back his hips to come outside her beautiful body. He shook from head to toe as he pumped into his fist. When he finally spurted his last drop, he was covered in sweat and shaking.

He set his forehead to her chest and breathed deep.

Amy embraced him lightly, uncaring that he was damp against her soft perfection. "Oh, sir."

Harper hugged her tight to him and squeezed his eyes shut. He might not want just a night with this woman. He could easily want far more. Not even Diana had inspired his passions to such a degree. He'd never made love to his late wife on top of a table.

And still he wanted Amy Mellish any way he could have her.

Guilt ate at him as he tidied himself. He'd had a good marriage and had never thought to feel so much again and certainly not with a stranger. However, he'd been wrong. A tiny slip of a woman had almost brought him to his knees in one brief interlude. Every nerve he possessed urged him to keep her near, no matter the cost to his pocket or his reputation.

He caught her lax hands in his and raised her to a seated position.

Amy met his gaze, her expression open and utterly trusting. She said nothing. She did not have to. He had more than pleased her tonight. He had shown her how lovemaking should be.

He brushed her again-tangled hair behind her shoulders. "Let us go to bed."

"I could easily sleep here," she said, blushing deeply.

"I'm sure you could, but there isn't a bed." He smiled. "I want you again. In my bedchamber, in my bed, and you will be far warmer I assure you and imminently more comfortable for what I have in mind for what's left of the night."

"What else is there to do?" She searched his face, uncertainty clear again.

"More of the same and perhaps even better pleasure if I'm very wicked and very devoted to you. I promise you that I do not intend to deny you anything you might desire tonight."

"I had no idea a man could feel so good." After a moment she nodded and slipped off the table. "I'd like to learn more of desire if you have the patience to show me."

With her fingers twined with his, he doused the candles and led her toward the stairs leading to his bedchamber. Harper intended to be a thorough teacher.

CHAPTER SIX

AMY PULLED her coat tightly around her body and strode into
the freshening gale. Despite the warm night that had just passed in
Mr. Cabot's fine arms, she was chilled through to the bone and
again desperate. She should have taken Mr. Cabot's money this
morning, but the sum he had left on top of her pile of clothes,
greater than discussed, had been too embarrassing to accept.

He had paid her far too much for the effort bedding him had
required on her part. Indeed, she had barely done more than lie
next to him before he was amorous again, touching her body with a
shockingly determined zeal that had lasted all evening until sleep
had finally claimed them both.

Amy had never been made love to before, and the sensations
had been so unexpectedly nice, consuming her mind even now,
hours after Mr. Cabot had last touched her. While it had been
happening, she had felt cherished for the first time in her adult
life.

She tossed her head, determined to put the rare night of pleasure from her mind and concentrate on what she needed to do

today. The chances of her next customer being anything like Mr. Cabot's fine passions were extremely remote.

Surely there would be a few gentlemen out that morning alone who wanted company. However, so far it seemed that the London shops were again overflowing with happily married couples who held tight to each other in the strong winds. No wandering eyes. No careful tilt of their heads to indicate they wanted to meet with her in less revealing locations like an alley or a nearby carriage. Yet again she was overlooked as a source of interest for that kind of man.

She stopped beside Harkness & Son, three blocks from Mr. Cabot's establishment, and pulled up her new fur-lined gloves while she considered whether it was time to leave Bond Street entirely. The only payment she had accepted from Mr. Cabot had been the warm gloves he had left beneath his generous payment. But they would not put a roof over her head or food in her belly unless she sold them, and she could not bear to part with the only reminder she would have of the nice Mr. Harper Cabot.

It was obvious he had his little peculiarities, but none had been a hardship. A bath and fresh fine cloth wrapped around her body had excited him. Why else would he have been so considerate and gentle and not thrown her out as soon as he was satisfied?

Today her fingers were not in danger of freezing and her stomach did not protest it was empty, so for the moment she was content. She was only pleasantly weary in body. Mr. Cabot had made love to her three times in total, rocking her body with such unusual sensations each time. Around midnight he had risen, brought food and drink to his bed, and fed her with his own fingers and glass. Afterward he had told her to rest. She had spent an awkward few moments in his arms until he had rolled over and fallen fast asleep first.

He had not even stirred when she had crept from his room as dawn broke.

She glanced up as an expensive-looking black carriage stopped before her. The wrinkled face of a woman appeared in the window and stared with keen interest. Amy knew no ladies in London and quickly pulled her scarf farther over her face, disturbed by the woman's interest in her.

The carriage moved on after a moment and she sighed.

It was definitely time to leave Bond Street if she had begun to attract the notice of amorous old women.

She stepped into the street again and hurried along before pausing at the Harkness window. A third-rate haberdashery shop if ever she had seen one except for the new window display. Harkness & Son had duplicated Mr. Cabot's current display window, right down to the sprigs of mistletoe lying between the assorted hats. The sight offended her.

Amy could not stand thieves, whether it be of riches or merely ideas.

Mr. Cabot had changed his windows last week, well before Harkness had, so she knew for a fact who was copying whom.

"See something you like?" a male voice asked.

Amy glanced into a young man's face. Mr. Harkness Jr.'s smile was insincere, and she shook her head, unwilling to engage him in conversation. She did not like the man. He gave her almost the same chilly feeling as the dangerous man she had met yesterday. She usually made a point of avoiding him. "No, thank you."

The man frowned. "You'd best return to your friends then. There's a killer on the prowl, don't you know?"

"A killer?" Amy squeaked.

"Indeed. They found a body not far from here," Mr. Harkness informed her with a disgruntled expression as he looked down the street. "He bled her and now no one is doing anything but talking about it. Bad for business. Very bad indeed."

Amy paled and her hands shook inside her new gloves. "Where?"

"Next lane along the street. Found her before she passed, but it was too late to do any good. She could not even describe the villain."

A dull roar filled her ears, and she trembled in earnest at hearing the location of the attack. She had been right there. At that very spot and had heard her call out for help. "Who was she?"

"A foolish light-skirts selling her favors." He nodded to a passing couple. "Doubt anyone will come looking for her, so I guess we will never know her name."

Amy's insides flipped. That could have been her dead in that alley too. She turned away and blindly hurried along the footpath as she fought to calm herself. Had she really met the killer? Had she almost been enticed into his clutches yesterday like that poor woman? She feared it was so. Thank God for her instincts. Thank God Mr. Cabot had let her escape into the safety of his home last night.

When the place of the murder drew close, her heart raced, and her palms grew slick inside her gloves. A crowd had gathered around the nearby shops. Amy did not dare stop to listen to what they might be saying or hear the girl's description bandied around. She might know of her.

She dodged through traffic to the other side of the road so she would not pass the site of the murder.

Regret that she had not taken Mr. Cabot's generous payment haunted her now. She'd like nothing better than to hide herself away in a snug little rented chamber for a few days to get over the shock. To hide from the fact that she had been one bad decision away from certain death.

Could she return to Mr. Cabot and reclaim his payment?

She was not sure if she was bold enough, but what harm could it do to see him again? At worst he might ignore her. She hurried onward, meeting the eye of several gentlemen but not encouraging their pursuit. She was too frightened to look at anyone longer than the time it took to confirm she was not about to run headlong into the killer.

Cabot's window loomed sooner than she expected, and to her relief the wonderfully improper Mr. Cabot stepped out onto the pavement. At his side was an elegant woman, her hand resting possessively on his arm. He waved up a carriage and very solicitously aided her inside it. They seemed to be on good terms, smiling and talking quietly, and when he kissed the back of her hand, Amy's courage withered.

She could not ask him for the money now. A man like Cabot would not want to be reminded of her, not when he had women of better class and accomplishments smiling like that at him. He could have any number of willing women throwing themselves in his direction, and now he was past the first awkward coupling after his wife's passing—if that was even true—he would scoop them up and eat them too, given the scope of his sexual appetite.

She dipped her chin as a blush warmed her cheeks at the memory of Mr. Cabot's passion, and skirted around them as quickly as she could, hoping not to be noticed and yet dreading that she would not be.

"Miss Mellish, good afternoon," Harper Cabot called urgently before she had gone a pace beyond his windows.

Amy turned back slowly, unable to hide her surprise at hearing her name on his lips. "Mr. Cabot."

"How very good to see you." He approached boldly; his expression guarded. "Might I enquire after your health? You seem pale."

"I am very well." She tried to control the shaking of her hands but could not manage it well. She did manage a weak smile. "Very well indeed."

He drew closer yet, and his touch ghosted over her elbow. "I looked for you this morning," he said quietly.

"Gents to meet, places to see," she murmured cheekily, aiming for a casual air that must have missed the mark by a wide margin judging by how his skin paled. When she realized how cold that might sound to her last lover, she blushed, ashamed of herself. She shook her head. "I did not meet with anyone else today."

He relaxed somewhat but seemed at a loss for what to say to that.

Desperate to fill the silence, Amy fell back on harmless pleasantries. "I trust you slept well last night."

"As I've not for a very long time. I wish I hadn't, for I intended to give you this." He dug in his pocket and a flash of silver winked at her from his fingers. "You must have missed seeing it on the table."

The coin had been on top of her clothes. She had held it only a moment before doing the right thing and setting it back on his table. "I saw it."

"But?" The coin disappeared back into his pocket. "Did you not think the payment fair?"

"It was too much. The food and lodgings and gloves were payment enough. The gloves especially are all I needed." She forced a smile and checked to see no one was close by. "If anything, I might owe you for the pleasure you bestowed upon me."

His eyes dilated with lust, and he gripped her elbow firmly. "I was well satisfied last night too. In fact, I'd like to feel that way again."

Amy smiled, her insides warming in a way a second tryst with the same customer usually did not cause. She discreetly pinched herself to check she was not dreaming. She might not have to find a lover tonight if she could make another business arrangement with Mr. Cabot. Something for something. Hopefully this time she might actually deserve to be paid. "That would be very agreeable."

A strong breeze whipped her cloak aside, and she shivered.

"Your hands are shaking."

"I'm quite warm in my new gloves." Indeed, conversation with Mr. Cabot and the discussion of last night's tryst had driven away much of her fear of the killer and the cold. "They are quite fine for ensuring my warmth."

"Poppycock. You should have kept the stockings too." He glanced around. "Come with me."

He began to urge her toward his shop front, but they hadn't gotten far when she dug in her heels before anyone noticed them. "No, sir. Not that way. I shouldn't."

His jaw set, clearly not liking her denial. "Very well. The rear entrance. Immediately."

"Yes, sir. A pleasure seeing you again," she murmured for the benefit of a passing couple staring at them as they passed. She dipped a curtsy to Mr. Cabot and made her way down the street in a happy bubble of excitement. Cabot's Haberdashery was in the middle of a long block. It would take her some time to reach the rear door, and by then she hoped to wipe the ridiculous smirk off her face. It was difficult though. A handsome, well-placed gentleman wanted to share his bed with her again. Perhaps her luck had finally changed for the better.

At the corner she glanced behind her. Mr. Cabot was waiting on the footpath outside his shop, facing her direction, watching her progress intently. His hand twitched in a half wave that she returned with a similarly small movement. She pressed her lips together to contain a smile and turned the corner, made her way along the icy footpath, and then stared into the grimy dimness of the lane behind his group of shops.

Had she truly intended to spend last night in this filthy place?

By the light of day, she was revolted as the night before had not made her feel. What if the killer had found her here last night? What if he was already waiting?

Her hands trembled anew, and her fright returned.

She moved quickly along the cobblestones, skirting refuse and worse. To her relief she spotted Mr. Cabot ahead. He had come out the back door without a hat on his head to wait for her arrival.

"Sir, you'll catch your death," she chided as soon as she reached him.

"If worrying about you doesn't send me off first." He urged her inside and slammed the door shut.

The heat in the room hit her and her eyes watered. She rushed to the hearth even as Mr. Cabot continued.

"Never, ever sneak away from my door without saying goodbye first."

She blinked at his tone and slowly turned around again. "Sir?"

"You didn't take my money. You didn't even make yourself tea or breakfast." He raked his hand through his hair. "For God's sake, what kind of coldhearted bastard do you take me for? Did you believe I could spend such a night with you and then toss you out into the cold?"

"I didn't think any of that. You are a kind man. Very decent." She took a step away from the fire, though she quickly discerned Mr. Cabot was only concerned rather than truly angry about her leaving the money behind. "I left quietly so that you would not be subjected to harmful gossip if I was seen leaving your shop this morning. I did not want anyone to wonder about who I was and where I was coming from."

"Pacing the street all morning and constantly peering out the front windows has ensured my reputation as a madman by now. Do you know there's a bloody killer on the loose?"

"I heard of the woman who died." She glanced at the rear door and saw it remained unlocked. Amy attended to that quickly. "I really am quite fine."

"You are still trembling." He drew close and set an arm about her waist. "I did not mean to lose my temper. I apologize. I know I have no right to scold you."

"It is not what you said." Amy leaned into him, at last feeling truly warm for the first time that day. "I met him. The killer I mean. At least I suspect I spoke to him yesterday."

"Where?"

"At the start of the lane where the woman was found. He wanted me, but there was something about him that made me afraid, so I pretended to be a proper lady and turned away."

Cabot crushed her against his chest. His palms stroked over her breasts and then lowered to her belly. "Do you know how lucky you are?"

"Yes." Amy closed her eyes as tears threatened. "If not for your inviting me in last night, he might have found me again. I don't know what I could have done but run away."

He kissed her cheek and then pressed a longer one to her skin. "I want your word that you will remain indoors until my workday is done."

"And then?"

He kissed the corner of her mouth, and she turned to face him. "We'll discuss payment for last night and tonight. Is that agreeable?"

Warmth pooled in her belly at the fierce desire in his eyes. "Yes, Mr. Cabot. I should like to stay with you very much indeed."

He kissed her properly then, something he had avoided doing last night.

It was brief but very thorough.

Her whole body came alight with delicious sensations that made her want to hold him against her and never let him go. He cupped her bottom and dragged her hips flush against his. Beneath his clothes, evidence of his desire prodded against her belly. Amy wriggled her hips, brushing against him until he growled against her lips.

Amy wrapped her arms about his shoulders and dreamed he would be the only man to ever kiss her. It was a pleasant fantasy but surely one that could never come true.

After a little while, he set her away from him. His trousers bulged with a keen erection and Amy bit her lip, loving that she could so easily arouse him.

He caught her amused smile and shook his head. "I kept food aside for you from the luncheon basket the baker sends me, in the hope that you would come back, and of course there is tea or wine in the larder if you prefer either one."

"Tea will be sufficient." Tea would warm both her insides and her hands as she held the cup.

She set her hands at his waist, struggling to control the desire burning through her body as she admired Mr. Cabot. If he asked, she would lift her skirts for him here and now and let him have his way as quickly as he liked.

She breathed deeply but all she could smell was the soap he had used last night. It was a comforting scent. It reminded her of home, but not any home she had lived in. Her mother had preferred pine and lemon, gathered from the nearby Brentwood fields. "Thank you for offering to shelter me again, Mr. Cabot. It is very decent of you."

He was not used to compliments, she could tell from the way his cheeks pinked, but his good humor returned as he smiled. "Until tonight, Miss Mellish."

She nodded and reluctantly stepped back from his warm presence and her own desire. "Until later, sir."

CHAPTER SEVEN

AS SOON AS his staff departed for the day, Harper sought Amy out and found her dozing by the fire in his kitchen. He breathed a heavy sigh of relief that she was still there. He had been plagued by worry all afternoon that he had not stressed enough the danger of venturing outside alone. Three female victims, all very similar to Amy—in desperate circumstance—had perished at the hands of an unknown assailant in the back alleys of Bond Street in recent weeks. The manhunt had little to go on and been unsuccessful so far.

That Amy remembered the man so well to be afraid of a mere memory had prevented him from asking immediately for a description. He had become so worried about her state of mind that he had actually considered closing the shop early to spend time with her.

"Mr. Cabot." Amy jerked upright, blinking sleep from her eyes.

"I did not mean to wake you."

She rubbed her eyes. "What time is it?"

"A little after five in the afternoon. My staff are long gone, and

I wondered if you'd like to keep me company as I tally the books for the day."

She stood quickly. "I would love to."

He led her toward the shop, settling his hand to her lower back as they walked side by side. The front blinds were already pulled down. They had as much privacy as could be wanted. "Welcome to my shop, Miss Mellish."

She glanced around, smiling with delight. "It is lovely."

Harper gestured Amy toward the rear room where he had work to do. He pulled on a pair of white gloves and straightened the expensive bolts of fabric. "This area contains the most expensive fabrics and goods we stock. It is by invitation only to protect the goods from overhandling that might soil them."

Amy looked at the items closely but kept her hands behind her back as if afraid to touch. "I can see why most women would covet an invitation to come in here. It's not just for the pleasure of having you all to themselves, is it?"

They were alone in the shop, but he could not seem to keep his possessiveness under control. The idea that Amy might have placed herself in further danger by leaving without payment infuriated him the longer he considered it. If she had stayed, if she had even taken his money, she might have spent the day safe from the murderous bastard lurking out there. He would not have had to worry or consider searching for her as night fell.

Her color was better now, and that brought relief. Earlier she had been so pale he feared a collapse until they had kissed. Realizing she had spoken to a killer must have been quite the shock. He was sure such a conversation would take some time for anyone to recover from.

"You give my appeal too much credit."

"Nonsense." She sighed. "I am certain most of your customers patronize the shop for the sole purpose of your company. Most women would welcome your advances."

"And yet I don't want that." He drew close to her and caressed her cheek, unable to stop checking that she was not trembling. "I hired Pelaw to provide a new direction for their flirtations. Hunter is much too cynical to attract anyone."

"Poor Mr. Cabot. So very hard done by that he must put up with daily flirtation." She laughed lightly and then glanced around, frowning. "So little has changed here. I remember this room from when I was a girl."

"Did you sneak in?"

"Oh no. Mother had to meet a customer here." Amy frowned again. "I recall no mention of an account."

"Only nobles hold accounts with us, and a few wives of prosperous local businessmen. Your mother must have been well favored. Our customers usually do not bring their dressmakers with them."

"The lady most likely could not have been bothered to make up her own mind." Amy traced a circle in midair above her head with her finger. "The strain of the title and all those heavy jewels they wear bear down on their brains to such a degree that such a simple decision-making is beyond their capabilities."

He looked at her in surprise. "Now you sound bitter."

"Do I?" Amy huffed. "Well, I have reason to be. All my life I have watched a long procession of self-important women order my mother and me around simply because they have funds to waste."

He knew the feeling well. "It is in the nature of the wealthy to demand much, but why were you singled out too?"

"Because we were poor, I suspect. There was no one to stop them from being rude either. There was one woman who liked me to present myself on each visit. Mother detested her but couldn't refuse so important a customer." She sighed deeply. "So, I was made to dress in my Sunday best on a Wednesday and recite long passages of her books to her."

"You can read and write?"

Amy nodded, her expression annoyed. "Poor, yet educated enough to know how far below everyone my irregular birth makes me, sir."

He held up his hands. "I didn't mean to offend. I just find it surprising. Most women of lower birth are never educated."

Amy finally picked up a length of lace and held it up to the light. "I had a tutor until my mother's death."

Had Amy's father been someone important? "Couldn't the tutor have helped you find a good situation?"

"A few nights after my mother passed away and was buried, my tutor helped himself to my virtue regardless of my disinterest in him or the activity." She wrinkled her nose. "Can we talk of something more pleasant?"

Good God. He wanted to kill whoever had forced her into his bed. "Certainly."

"Where do you get your buttons?" She moved to the door and stepped out into the storefront. "As a child I was always fascinated by their many and varied shapes. My mother kept a very small collection, but you have so many more on display than I can believe exist."

"A great many places." He followed her out to the button display, growing aroused by the gentle sway of her hips as she moved. He stopped beside the buttons and placed one hand at the small of her back again while he described them. "This one was sent to me by a German, this one is from France and has been hard to replace of late, and this one here comes all the way from the Canary Islands. It is made from a particularly rare seashell. I have made a great many acquaintances over the years, and they always keep an eye out for the extraordinary."

Her fingers ghosted over the jars. "Do you always keep them so mixed?"

"They were sorted yesterday."

She looked more closely and then appeared flustered. "My mistake."

Harper looked again and swore under his breath. "I should employ your good eyes to straighten Mr. Pelaw out. They are indeed mixed. Can he not tell wood from heavy shell?"

Amy moved one to a different jar, then pulled another from the same jar and placed it aside while she looked for a match in the other jars. "He sorts by color, not by the material they are made from. May I fix this for you?"

"I would appreciate that, but first..." He snapped her stockings from his pocket with a flourish. "You seem to have misplaced your new, warmer stockings."

He knelt, removed her worn boots and stockings, and slipped the new pair up her slim legs. He tied them in place with blue garters this time and kissed the inside of each knee. "I meant for you to keep them too."

"They are too fine for my life out there."

Her response saddened him. He stood, caught her face in his hand, and kissed her lips. He had denied himself the pleasure of her lips last night because they had seemed red and chafed and had regretted it come morning when he found his bed empty and her long gone.

He moved back. "I have to attend the window display."

"No doubt Harkness & Son will copy any changes you make by luncheon tomorrow," she grumbled sourly as she tucked her legs beneath her chair. "If not before."

"What was that?" He kneeled again and replaced her worn boots on her slender feet for want of something better. "Are they copying me again?"

Amy nodded, a disgusted look on her features as their gaze met. "Their mistletoe isn't as fresh, but their display seems exactly the same to me in every other aspect."

"Damn them. Every year they do this." He tugged his hand through his hair, uncertain it was worth the effort of making any changes so close to the holiday.

Amy worried at her lower lip but then smiled. "May I make a suggestion?"

"You have an idea of how to beat them?"

"Not exactly beat them but..." She bit her lip. "You should dispense with the display entirely."

He shook his head. "A bare window does not attract customers."

"It is cold, sir. If anyone is out in this dreadful weather, they are most certainly going to come inside. You just have to give them a reason to stay."

"I don't understand." He leaned against the table, enjoying their talk immensely. "A window display is done to entice them inside."

"To stand around as if waiting for a dancing partner? I know little about the running of a shop, but what might adding comfortable chairs and a small table to each bay window, just like White's, do for your business?" She smiled. "Serve coffee and offer a plate of ginger biscuits for the husbands."

"Husbands?"

"Bond Street was awash with couples today and yesterday too. If the gentlemen do not feel welcome, they will lure their wives away too soon without allowing them the time to purchase their heart's desire. But if they were to be made as welcome as can be, their wives would be free to see and consider whatever they might like at a leisurely pace. They would not rush back outside at all."

"Oh," he whispered, staring at her with renewed respect as he pictured the scene she painted. "Oh, my. That is a very good idea. My dear, you are full of surprises. I think we shall try that."

He kissed her soundly, then spent the next hour rearranging the front of his shop to accommodate her suggestion, stealing two small tables and lace tablecloths from his own quarters to set the scene. When he was done, he smiled at Miss Mellish only to find her studying her fingers as if she felt out of place without his attention.

He knew exactly how to jolly her out of that feeling.

CHAPTER EIGHT

HARPER CABOT STROKED her hair so confidently that Amy was swept with gooseflesh.

"How is that?" he asked, his voice husky against her ear.

"Mr. Cabot, you spoil me." Amy wiggled her toes toward the fire, eager to feel the delightful heat against her stocking-covered feet. They were seated in his sitting room above the haberdashery as if they were the best of friends and not the prostitute and shop-keeper, which they most definitely were. Harper had the chair while Amy sat on the thick floor rug, leaning against his knees, as close to the fire as it was possible to get without burning herself.

"I think it's past time someone did," he suggested.

She shivered and not from the cold. This time with Harper was a temporary peace in a futile future for her. The realization that such tender moments were fleeting made her sad down to the bone. Despite the heaviness of her soul, she strove for a light tone so as not to concern him. "I can't remember how long it's been since I've been so warm."

Harper sipped his port and then set it aside. He was a slow drinker, savoring the flavor rather than allowing himself to become foxed as many men were wont to do on a cold winter's night. "What was your life like before your mother died?"

His question, like so many before it, brought discomfort. She took a very small sip of her port, mostly to keep him company. "Pleasant. We had a small house on the edge of Brentwood. Mother was all I had. She was a seamstress and made beautiful gowns, but never any for herself. I was the best-dressed outcast in Essex."

"Is that so?"

"Sad but true. I grew up at her feet surrounded by pins and threads and luxurious fabrics. I had a silk pillow once and a velvet muffler made of scraps from other people's gowns. It never occurred to me that she would die so young. There was so much I wish we'd talked about now."

He stroked her hair again. He had taken it down after dinner and seemed to like running his fingers through the dark strands quite a lot. "I felt the same when my wife died. She promised she was feeling better, and like a fool I believed her. I thought we had forever. I should have spent more time with her."

Amy leaned her head against Mr. Cabot's knee and sighed.

Cabot leaned forward and pressed his lips to the top of her head. "Are you still comfortable there?"

"There is a fire burning, Mr. Cabot, and I am warm," she said. "That is really all it takes to make me happy."

"We could always turn in." He stood, took his glass and hers to the sideboard. "Were you warm enough last night?"

"Everything about last night was perfect, sir." Amy twisted around to keep him in view. A smile curved his generous lips, and it struck Amy anew just how considerate he was. Her body quivered a little at the memory of his mouth and tongue tasting her intimately. Of his body hovering over hers without crushing her. Of his questions and soft laughter as she had expressed her wonder at her astonishing reactions to his caresses. She would like to feel so cherished again, but had no notion of how to ask in a way that did not sound vulgar.

"Indeed, it was." He sighed. "Come to bed, Miss Mellish."

Amy climbed to her feet after casting a reluctant glance at the fireplace and followed him into the adjoining room.

Mr. Cabot's bedchamber was already warm, a cheerful fire burned, and the wide bed was inviting and probably as soft she remembered. She undid one button of her gown and glanced around. Last night the room had not been so well lit when they had come up, and now she saw what the shadows of full dark had concealed.

A woman's possessions were scattered all about the room. Cosmetics were piled up on the dressing table, satin slippers and a robe strewn over a chair. A collection of hatboxes were stacked beneath a high window and were covered in pretty, feminine fabric.

It was as if the late Mrs. Cabot might return at any moment.

The thought made Amy decidedly uncomfortable and chilled her heart. Mr. Cabot had not packed away any of his wife's possessions. He was still grieving for the woman he had loved and lost so suddenly. She faced him quickly, noting that Mrs. Cabot's possessions existed only on one side of the room. Amy liked the view of Mr. Cabot's possessions so much better. She felt less an intruder facing that direction.

She moved toward Cabot quickly and stopped at his side.

He peered into her face, the warm light in his eyes slowly fading as their eyes held. "Is something the matter?"

"No." Amy brought her hands to his cravat and frowned at the complicated knot. How to untie it defeated her. "What is this knot called?"

"A Cabot. It is my own design." He lifted his chin and began to untie it. "So, are you well versed in knotting, too?"

"No." She concentrated on the twisting's and turning's of the complicated knot until it gave way. "I only know how to unravel them."

Amy stretched the long length of cloth and then laid it over a chair back close to the fire. She wriggled a little in the warmth the fire cast on her skin. Fires were wonderful creations. She'd never take them for granted again.

She jumped as Harper grasped her hips from behind.

"Stay there." He made short work of removing her gown and then, after another rustle of fabric, fell to his knees behind her. "Hold on to the mantel if need be."

His lips brushed the top of her bottom, and then he slowly moved lower, kissing her cheeks and thighs lightly as he went. He eased his fingers around her inner thighs and applied pressure until she parted her legs.

He rested his face against her side. "You are so soft and lovely to touch."

Amy squirmed as he probed between her legs and then penetrated her sex with his fingers. She was not used to such attention but soon moaned at everything he did. He worked his fingers in and out of her sheath until she was panting, gripping the mantel for support as her bones turned to water. He was doing it again, driving her toward a pleasure only he'd shown her. His touch was setting her nerves on fire, but she knew his cock would feel so much better.

"Sir, please."

"Please what, Miss Mellish?"

Amy threw her head back, allowing her long hair to brush her bottom. She widened her stance. "Please be inside me."

He thrust into her with his fingers and then pushed a little deeper until she moaned. "I am inside you."

"Not like that." She groaned as he teased forward to her clitoris and circled the spot. "I want you."

"What do you want, and be precise now," he said, a hint of laughter in his tone.

She blushed. "I want your cock inside me. I want you to be wicked with me."

"That is exactly what I hoped you'd say." He embraced her from behind, and the hard length of his erection branded her bottom. He had removed his clothes at some point without her realizing he was naked too. She turned to view him, curious about what else the darkness of last night had concealed.

Harper was generously proportioned—wide shoulders, narrow hips, thick of cock but not so big as to hurt her. Seed wept from the tip, and Amy licked her lips, anticipating another pleasure she was sure he would like to receive from her.

Harper caught her up in his arms and carried her toward the bed before she could fall to her knees and take him into her mouth. He eased her down on his side of the mattress, parted her legs, and then settled over her.

Amy pressed her hands to his chest, prepared for the first thrust and the ones to come. He did not move. "Sir?"

Instead of sliding into her body immediately, he touched her all over—her hips, her thighs, her breasts, which he cupped and kissed until she was breathless. When he did ease into her body, she was desperate for release.

"Oh, my dear lady," he whispered. "You feel so very good around me."

Amy blushed and wrapped her arms about his neck, holding on to him as he began to move in earnest. Being loved by Mr.

Cabot was no chore, no imposition. She could not be paid for accepting such beautiful feelings.

Amy kissed him, teased his tongue with hers, and wrapped her fingers about the back of his neck to hold him close.

It seemed that every time with Harper was like the first time she had made love to him. She slid her hands up and down his sides, pulling him deeper into her body, harder against her skin. Making love was lovely, a fine dance with only their desire making music.

Amy brought her knees up to his chest and then slipped one over his shoulder. The higher angle of thrust brought a moan tumbling from his lips. He glanced down at where they joined. "Damn, but that is an incredible view."

He slowed his thrusts, and Amy craned her neck to see them join. She ached anew as his wet length slid out.

"Come back," she whispered and was rewarded with his slow return. The shocking thrill, the glide of his flesh into hers, was beyond her experience. Amy closed her eyes as he repeated the slow penetration.

Cabot rotated his hips, moving his cock in a slow circle inside her body. Amy grasped his arms as she was assailed by a riot of sensations she could not deny. She dug her fingers into his firm flesh even as her body came apart from the sudden change in friction. She shrieked as pleasure spiked and kept her eyes closed as Harper pounded her body only to groan a moment later, spilling his seed inside her body.

She opened her eyes slowly and met his. Her heart flipped at his warm expression.

He cupped her face and then kissed her soundly. "Glorious."

"Indeed," she whispered, meaning his passions. There seemed no end to Harper's desire and no barrier to sharing new and exciting experiences with him.

Lust like this had no price. Amy could not accept payment for what they shared in this bed, in this place of business. Not when she was the one who was receiving so much more pleasure than she was giving out. It was supposed to be a business arrangement between them but taking money would cheapen what she felt when they were together.

CHAPTER NINE

HARPER WOKE SUDDENLY AND COMPLETELY, memories of last night's passionate hours clear and arousing. He reached for Amy as she rose stealthily from his warm bed. "Sneaking away again?"

"I hate partings," she whispered. However, she settled on the edge of the bed with a heavy sigh and made no further move to leave him.

He scooted across the bed to capture her. "Then stay here today. The snow is falling thick outside."

He had no idea if that was true or not, but it was his only excuse for selfishness. She should not be outside in the elements. Not alone. She needed shelter, and Harper was keen to keep her warm and comfortable.

Amy glanced at the window and her face fell. "That is terrible news."

"Is it really an imposition?" He smiled at her and teased her arm. Last night had been more than pleasurable. More satisfying than the night before. He wanted a chance to feel that way again, but only with Amy. If she was willing to remain as his guest and lover. "Stay here. Stay warm and don't go out."

There was also the danger of a killer who had not been caught to worry about. He had managed to pass along Amy's halting description yesterday without saying where he had gathered the information from. He hoped they caught the man soon.

He would mention the threat the killer posed only if she was determined to leave. He could not bear to see her shake in fear again.

She drew in a sharp breath and glanced around. He believed her tempted. Who wouldn't be prepared to stay in when the winter devils were howling around the eaves? "Well, if you want me, I can certainly keep you entertained."

"Pleasure will have to wait until tonight. As much as I would like to remain abed with you, I have the shop to run still, and your clever idea to put into motion," he reminded her. "Aside from the start of the season, this is the busiest time of year for the shop. You would not believe the excuses women use to explain the purchase of twenty yards of lace and silk to match."

"Oh, I can indeed imagine. My mother barely slept at this time of year, finishing gowns for the wealthiest ladies of our town. They probably wore them for just a few hours too." She nibbled on her lip. "If you will not need me for pleasure, do you have anything for me to do for the day? A bath, a warm bed, and so much food must be repaid in kind. I must earn my keep."

He shifted closer to her and ran his hand up her spine. She sighed with pleasure. He loved that she reacted to every touch as if it was the best feeling she had ever experienced. "I had considered it a fair trade."

"You are too easy on me, sir. A few shillings worth of pleasure hardly compares for all you have done for me. It is *I* who owes you for all your kindness and the roof over my head. I have not been so wanted for months."

He frowned at the mention of the manner she earned her living and released her. It irritated him that other men had taken their pleasure with her and never considered her needs too. She was too good for that sordid use. Too gentle to have fallen so far with no one to protect her. Perhaps he could... He leaned against the headboard as the rest of that thought vanished before he could grasp it.

Besides, what had he done but use her as other men had before him?

Except, she had not taken a penny in coin for the pleasure her body had brought him. Indeed, their negotiations tended to fall by the wayside as soon as they touched. But there was also the satis-faction of her company to consider, and that was beyond any price he could name. Amy was bright, curious, and quite intelligent. An easy companion to share the evening with.

She had beaten back his loneliness with her sweet kisses and shared confidences. Having a woman to care for had lightened his heart to a considerable degree. "I have some shirts that are missing buttons. Perhaps, if it is not too much trouble, you might mend them?"

"Gladly. Might I do anything else for you before you start your workday?" She slid onto the bed and peeled the warm bedclothes away from his body. Since he had slept naked, she noticed his aroused state immediately. "A personal service, perhaps?"

He gasped as she took him in hand, and when her mouth closed around the head of his cock and she tongued his slit, his hips jerked off the bed. He came fully erect almost as soon as her head bobbed up and down.

Perhaps he would have to start work late that day.

It had been an age since a woman had done this to him, even

his wife had avoided the task in the past few years. Amy, however, was both attentive and vigorous in stirring his passions. He'd no idea she would want to do this. She moved onto her knees and her pert bottom wiggled in the air as she lavished him with every scrap of her attention. She sucked, her thin cheeks hollowing, and forced him very deep indeed. His heart almost stopped when she swallowed. He cupped her face as she massaged his cock head with the back of her throat.

"Dear God. That feels incredible," he whispered. "Where did you learn? No, do not answer that. I don't need to know."

Amy chuckled around him.

He grasped the nightgown he had slipped her into last night before exhaustion had claimed them and exposed her pale bottom. Amy wiggled just a little closer, offering her skin to his wandering hands. He stroked over her rear, skimming the tips of his fingers over her quim and back up again. She was delightfully moist as he probed her entrance, and he was eager to bring her pleasure too. As he pushed his fingers deep and twisted them, scissoring in the way she had liked last night, Amy hummed around his erection. Harper almost lost control and spilled down her throat there and then.

Only an intense need to hold her in his arms as he came prevented that.

Harper removed her mouth from his length and brought her pouting red lips to his. He kissed her deeply and hungrily, amused by her obvious disappointment at his interference. Amy came to rest over his body, restlessly rubbing against him. He sucked her tongue and then plundered her mouth with his own. Her thin limbs slid over his in a heady dance of sensation. He had missed morning trysts, though the feel of Amy was muted by her prim nightgown.

He removed it completely, so she was as naked as he and pulled her hard against him.

After a second thought he sat up, wrapping her legs around his waist and stroking along her spine while he suppressed his arousal. Amy might be tiny, but she was so very vivid and alert to his needs and appetites. To think he had almost hesitated to invite her into his home. He could not get enough of touching her and hearing her moan when he did.

She twisted up and brought him into her body.

Harper curled his arms around her back and rested his hands on her shoulders as he pressed her fully down until she could take no more. He held her close for a moment, loving the feeling of being connected again to another human soul whose desire for him was so patently obvious.

He eased back to play with her breast, catching her eye as he thumbed her nipple. "This is what you missed yesterday morning. We should start all our days together like this."

Amy moaned her agreement and shifted on his length. He lowered his hand to her quim and stroked the hard nubbin at the apex of her thighs.

She moaned loudly. "Oh, sir. Yes!"

He kissed her neck and then scraped his teeth over her pale flesh as he continued to tease her. "Harper," he whispered. "Call me Harper when we are abed."

"Harper, oh please do not stop touching me like that," she whispered as she writhed and squirmed, pushing into his teasing fingers, sliding his cock up and down her soaked passage. It was plain to see that she loved everything he did to her and saw no reason to hide her enjoyment.

Neither did he.

When she cried out, Harper rolled Amy onto her back and moved over her. He lifted her legs up onto his shoulders and drove into her again and again. Beneath him, Amy smiled with a dreamy quality, and he was incapable of looking away. He pounded her pussy until his balls drew up and he shot his seed deep inside with a hoarse shout.

At that moment, the bed gave an alarming groan and pitched against the wall.

Amy stared at him and then covered her mouth. "You broke the bed," she announced in a muffled voice.

He was breathing hard from his release but had energy enough to laugh. He had never done such a thing before, but he was not the only one to blame. He checked they were in no danger of complete collapse, then cupped her cheek. "*We* broke the bed. I wasn't the only one in it, so you must take a share of the blame."

She fought a grin to whisper, "I'm sorry."

"False contrition if ever I've seen it." He brushed his fingers over her temple and smoothed her dark hair over the white pillow. She was so lovely that for a moment his heart gave a queer lurch. He licked his lips. "Don't be sorry. Being loved is the best way to start the day in my opinion."

It was true; loving a woman was all he had ever wanted. And he had Amy for the moment. A woman he thought he might like to keep entirely for himself no matter how inappropriate the situation.

He would have to carefully consider how to keep a lover secret from his employees and sister. They each had an annoying habit of concerning themselves with Harper's love life. He did not want Amy scared away under any circumstances. Not when they had only just begun to explore their mutual desire.

CHAPTER TEN

AMY PEEKED through the gap in the doorway between Mr. Cabot's private residence and the bustling haberdashery. She was bored and restless; she had not seen Mr. Cabot's face for over an hour since he had disappeared into the far room with a haughty-looking woman and had closed the door. The room held his best fabrics and undoubtedly he was being his usual attentive self to another lady.

That idea was entirely bothersome.

She eased the door open a tiny bit more to observe the pair of gentlemen drinking coffee and munching on ginger biscuits in the bay windows. Her idea seemed to be working, but she was not sure if her suggestion was adding to Mr. Cabot's sales.

Noticing the plate of ginger biscuits had fallen to just one again, she carefully closed the door and turned to the worktable to prepare a fresh plate for Mr. Cabot to collect the moment he noticed it was needed. When it was done, she sat down again and worried at her lower lip, considering how she might be more helpful.

She was not used to being idle. Even as poor as she had been, Amy had made sure never to linger too long in any one place.

The shirts he had asked to be mended were done long ago. She had found a gentlemen's magazine on his night table but had found little in it to interest her. She had crept downstairs to the kitchen and found a full wicker basket of food for Mr. Cabot that must have been delivered during her brief exploration of the upper floor. She had set the table and laid out his luncheon in readiness. However, she had no idea how to attract his attention short of bursting in where a woman of her sort was not wanted.

She went back to her spot by the door. The clock struck the hour of one o'clock, and the older employee, Mr. Hunter, moved toward the front door. Whenever Amy had risked peeking into the shop, she had taken the time to study both men unobserved. Hunter was not as warm as Mr. Cabot but knew his yards and muslins and lace very well indeed. He turned every inquiry into a sale of something. He was liked but not flirted with as often as the ladies did with Mr. Cabot or Mr. Pelaw.

The younger man was the complete opposite of Hunter, politely completing purchases for his customers, offering up a sweet treat wrapped in festive paper as they left with a warm smile. A good portion of the women he served were falling in love with him already. The other half would be convinced soon enough given how sweet his manners. His handsome face was indeed a growing attraction for those patronizing Cabot's Haberdashery.

Amy, however, was more interested in Mr. Cabot—Harper— and the many and varied ways he could express his feelings without words. His tone of voice and posture spoke so loudly of his state of mind. Whether it be gentle persuasion to purchase or debate over a conflict of two choices, he was always kind and perceptive. He presented his interest with an intimacy that had caused more than one lady to smile intently at his retreating back.

However, to Amy's immense relief, she had seen no sign he wanted to be scrutinized so closely by those wealthy women.

He seemed oblivious to his appeal, which seemed utterly ridiculous. His presence, his body hard against hers, was a constant wish even now. Amy craved his fingers on her body, his cock sliding inside. For the first time in her life, she'd enjoyed being had by a gentleman as many times as he liked. She wanted him to want her just as badly.

Harper reappeared with his customer at last, escorting her past the sales counter and directly to the door. He was gone a few moments and then returned to the cutting table, his expression serious as he perused the empty shop.

"I would say we are in for a busy afternoon," the young assistant claimed as he returned to the sales counter too. "What a boon it is to have a few more men around the place. Their wives have been so happy with you for making that cunning arrangement of chairs."

"Yes, I did notice an increase in their enjoyment to have their husbands taken care of." Harper smiled. "Best be off on your errand now. Purchase double of this morning's order. I will need you back as soon as you are able."

"Thank you, sir. I won't be long." The man hurried away and slipped through the front door.

"You're too soft on him," Hunter grumbled.

"He is an excellent antidote for your cynicism," Harper stated and then laughed. "He stays."

"So now the lad has gone, are you going to tell me what happened last night?"

"Nothing happened last night."

"Bollocks." Hunter planted his feet and crossed his arms over his chest. "You look so positively pleased with yourself I could swear Diana was still alive. You've finally treated yourself to a bit o' muslin."

Amy shrank a little as Mr. Cabot remained silent a very long moment. He sighed. "Don't you have somewhere to be?"

"Indeed, I do." Hunter slapped his hat on his head, wrapped a scarf around his neck. "But I go utterly happy that my friend had a very good night, even if he won't admit to it."

The door shut with a loud bang.

Amy turned her attention back to *her gentleman* only to find Harper watching her with keen eyes. "You can come out and stop spying on me now."

Amy eased her way into the shop uncertainly. "I didn't mean to be noticed."

"And you were not by anyone but me." He strode for the front door, locked it, and then returned, a slight hitch in his step as he drew near. He caught her about the waist and twirled her around. His smile was blinding. "I was thinking of you and there you were. Your idea is a great success. We have already had a day's worth of sales and it is only just midday."

"I am so glad." She smiled shyly. "I could not determine if you were happy or not. I finished your shirts."

"Oh," he said, smiling before pressing his lips to her temple and slowly kissing his way to her sensitive neck. She shuddered as he grazed his teeth over her skin. When he spoke, his voice had a husky bedroom inflection. "What else have you done? Did you curl up by the fire or attempt to fix my broken bed?"

"Neither." She took his hand and tugged. "Come. You should eat."

He allowed her to lead him to his private residence, but he paused on the threshold of the kitchen and surveyed what she had done with his table. "Where did you find the food for all this?"

"In your daily basket from the baker and in the cupboards too.

There were a goodly number of preserves to choose from and other tasty items you must like. 'Tis a very well-stocked larder you have, sir."

"You know, Pelaw remarked he could smell something earlier, and I dismissed it as his attempt to find an excuse to slip out for more tarts from the bakery across the street." He frowned. "My wife often used to bake during the day. She claimed the smell of food kept the customers buying."

Amy held a chair out for him, but his mention of his wife brought unexpected pain. He had loved his wife deeply. "You miss her."

"I have done." He glanced at her quickly and caught her hand. He brought it to his lips and pressed a kiss to her knuckles. "That is not to say I am unhappy you are here now. The snow continues to fall."

"I had noticed that too." She poured him tea and sat opposite him. "Thank you for allowing me to stay today."

"I heard the killer has not been apprehended." Mr. Cabot sipped his tea. He took it black, without adding sugar to it. "Stay tomorrow as well."

"Sir," she chided, although pleased to be asked. Another night in his arms, in his bed, would be very pleasant. She would love to stay, but such an arrangement was unwise. "As much as I would love to stay, shouldn't you be careful about keeping a woman like me around? There could be harmful gossip if I am discovered and, killer on the loose or not, doting mothers might abandon their patronage of your shop. If it became known you kept a fallen woman in your establishment, your reputation might suffer for it."

He grunted, a mulish expression darkening his handsome face.

"You know I am right, but I do thank you for your hospitality."

"It is too dangerous to let you go yet. What if the killer is waiting for you out there?" He glanced at her sternly. "You saw him clearly, didn't you?"

Amy nodded, heart sinking. "And he saw me."

Harper sat back in his chair, a worried frown on his face. "You had best stay out of sight until the trouble has passed. We will tell anyone who asks about you that you are my housekeeper."

"Would anyone believe me a housekeeper?"

"Let us hope so." He scraped a hand through his hair. "Oh, Amy, I am so tired of being alone, and I worry for you."

Amy shifted in her chair, attuned to that feeling of acute loneliness for so long that she accepted it would always be that way. She was tempted by his offer. "Where would I sleep?"

"With me abovestairs."

To have Harper's body wrapped around hers on these cold winter nights seemed a dream come true, but it was not possible. He had not packed away his wife's things yet, and she could not bear to spend too much time thinking about her. While Diana Cabot's gloves and hats lay strewn about his bedchamber, she would feel like an interloper in that room. "I should have my own room as any respectable housekeeper might expect to have."

He considered that a moment and then stood. "Very well, you can have a room, but I highly doubt you'll spend any time there."

He caught her hand and towed her toward the larder. She followed him in and blinked as he pushed on the end wall, revealing a doorway she had not realized was hidden away. "This was once a servant's room. The window was boarded up years ago, and it is tiny."

"No doubt larger and more comfortable than the last home I made for myself behind your shop," she said, smiling as she recalled her makeshift crate construction where he had found her two nights ago. The boxes had been taken away the day before, so she could not go back.

Amy eased past Harper and glanced around the space. It was bare and dusty, with a bed just big enough for one and an overturned crate as a nightstand. But it was dry and private, dark, which was all a servant could expect from any employer. It would be all hers, with no shadows of the late Mrs. Cabot looming over her head. Being Mr. Cabot's housekeeper would be far better than peddling her body on the cold of London's streets. However, if Harper wanted her body, she would gladly give herself to him whenever he liked. "It will do."

He appeared surprised. "I will introduce you to Mr. Hunter and Pelaw when they come back so you need not hide behind doors anymore."

She beamed. "Then let's get you back to your luncheon before then, and I will make a start on being an excellent housekeeper."

Harper drew her against him and kissed her soundly. "I like how you look after me already."

She fiddled with the ends of his cravat. "You looked out for me too, so it's a fair exchange."

"Indeed."

He took her lips in a slow, drugging kiss that made her toes curl in her new slippers. Harper had given her so much—his time, his attention, his hard body that made her feel so much. She slid her hand down to his bottom and squeezed.

He broke the kiss, panting. "Upstairs. I need to fuck you more than eat."

Amy laughed, hitched her skirts, and ran for his sitting room. She bent over his chair, and when she heard his heavy steps behind her, she wiggled her bottom. "Quick and quiet?"

He was silent, and Amy looked back over her shoulder. Harper had his cock in hand, stoking the hard length as he stared.

Amy tossed her skirts up to expose her bottom. She parted her legs and fingered her slit. She was already wet from his kisses, and she sighed at how excited she felt yet again. "Please. Hurry before your staff return."

Harper closed the distance between them, grasped her hips, and shoved into her waiting quim. "Fuck yes," he groaned as he withdrew and began to fuck her hard and fast. "You are so good for me, sweet Amy. We are so alike it frightens me."

Amy braced her hands on the chair, let her head fall forward as Harper shattered her senses. What she felt with Harper did not frighten her. She reveled in his attention because such pleasure could not possibly come her way again.

CHAPTER ELEVEN

INTRODUCING Amy to his staff was a moment of awkwardness Harper never wanted to experience again. The young Pelaw fell in love with her on first meeting. He gallantly took her hand and offered to fetch and carry anything she might need help with as the new housekeeper. Harper gritted his teeth. He would do any fetching and carrying for his lover-turned-housekeeper if there was any need, thank you very much. Not that he expected her to be keeping house; she was much too precious for that tedious chore.

Hunter saw through the ruse immediately and shook his head before turning away.

"Go ahead and open up." Harper propelled Pelaw toward the shop front a quarter hour earlier than planned just to get rid of him. "If he bothers you, I'll deal with him," he told Amy firmly.

Amy appeared surprised by his words but then nodded. "Indeed, I will, Mr. Cabot. I have no intention of being a distraction or encouraging your staff. You, however..."

"What about me?"

"Well, you are the reason I am here, so perhaps I could distract and encourage you from time to time." She smiled impishly. "May I bring you tea later?"

"Thank you. I would appreciate that."

She crooked her fingers and stepped backward from view of the shop with an anticipatory smile on her lips. Harper checked if Pelaw and Hunter were suitably occupied, then followed. He pressed Amy to the nearest wall and kissed her soundly.

"Hmm," she whispered as he drew back. "You could do that all day and I'd never complain."

He took a deep breath. He did not say it too, but he felt the same. There was something vastly satisfying about kissing the tiny woman witless that he half did not care who saw what they did together—except that it would matter to his customers and damage Amy's reputation. For now, she would be known as a respectable housekeeper. He just hoped he could keep his hands to himself long enough to convince everyone else it was true. If the truth did come out, he would be considered a scoundrel to be seducing a servant in his employ. He doubted he could turn off the attraction he felt for her so quickly. It would take time to douse this fire, and he was not entirely sure he did not want it to continue to burn. "Until later."

"I'll be ready and waiting." Her eyes glittered with desire.

He took a breath and eased closer. "For this to work, you might not want to look at me like that."

"Like what, sir?"

"Like you can't wait for me to part your thighs and ravish you on my bed."

Amy blushed but laughed softly. "Only you have ever made me wish for that."

"I truly hope so." He touched her burning-hot cheek, and satisfied, he strode into the shop and surveyed his domain. His body was filled with equal parts of anticipation and dread.

He took a deep breath as he imagined what he would do to her that night if he could wait that long. He was already wanting. By nightfall, he would be bloody impatient to hear her moan his name again.

"My dear Mr. Cabot," a woman demanded. "You are wool-gathering."

He glanced up quickly. "Lady Templeton! What an unexpected pleasure. I had not heard you'd returned to London."

"A pressing family matter brings me back."

Harper hurried around the counter and bowed. It did not pay to disappoint a countess, and especially not the Duke of Rutherford's daughter-in-law. "How may I help you today?"

The countess waved her hand. "A chair and tea."

"Of course," he agreed. Lady Templeton was a valued customer but always conducted her business, purchases for her daughters and nieces, in the private room. "I'll have my new housekeeper attend you."

He hurried to the kitchens and opened one set of cupboard doors. "Tea, best China, four sugar biscuits, and a bowl of sugar, no milk, silver tray. You will find everything you need in this cupboard, Amy, and be as quick as possible."

"I will."

He hurried back to the countess. "Sorry for the delay."

The countess waved her hand. "So, you've finally engaged a woman to serve. I do hope she has some talent for the task."

Harper nodded, but he was not entirely sure. "I'm confident she will do very well."

Actually, he prayed Amy did. Lady Templeton had spent a fortune in his business, much to his amazement. Pleasing her was important.

He glanced at the door and held his breath as Amy appeared carrying the silver tray. Her pace was steady, her demeanor perfectly submissive for a servant. She set everything out with steady hands and then turned around to curtsy to the countess.

Lady Templeton gasped, her hand fluttering to her throat. Her eyes widened at the sight of his lover. "I cannot believe it."

Amy took one look at the woman and paled. She dipped a second, deeper curtsy, one worthy of a court appointment. "My lady."

"You should not be here," Lady Templeton exclaimed. "Go and pack your things this instant."

"My lady!" Title or no, Harper did not care for her meddling in his affairs. "How dare you speak so to my newest employee?"

Amy fled for the kitchen with a strangled gasp while the countess took a turn, almost sliding out of her chair in distress.

Furious, Harper grasped the smelling salts he kept in a drawer for such emergencies and waved them under her nose. "My Lady Templeton. Damn it all. Pelaw, call up the countess's carriage. She is in need of a doctor."

"I don't need a doctor, you fool." The duchess clutched his arm. "Not a word of this, or I will ruin you."

He blinked at the fury in her tone but helped her stand. He escorted her out to the empty store, but the countess stopped before entering. "Fetch her at once."

"Fetch who?" Hunter asked, strolling closer with his brows raised.

The countess glowered. "That woman."

"There's no woman here but you, my lady." Hunter spread his arms wide as if proving it. The shop was thankfully empty of any who would gossip about this situation.

Lady Templeton glanced around them, eyes narrowed. "You will regret this, Mr. Cabot."

"I might if I knew the cause for your sudden distress."

Lady Templeton did not elaborate. Her lips pressed together

in a tight, worried line. She strode for the front door, and Harper raced to hold it open for her. As she crossed the threshold, her expression smoothed into a sweet smile. She allowed him to lead her to the waiting carriage and hand her in. Before the door closed, she whispered, "I will have my way, Mr. Cabot. Mark my words well, I will be back for the girl, and you would be wise not to stand in my way."

Harper blinked. "What the devil is going on?"

"Ask her," Lady Templeton said. "She did this to embarrass us all."

The carriage lurched forward, leaving Harper standing in the falling snow, utterly confused. He turned back to the shop and hurried inside. He would get the truth from Amy about her association with Lady Templeton before any damage was done to the shop's reputation.

However, he pulled up short as he spied his younger sister, Thallia Wayland, standing about with Hunter.

"Harpie, darling," she gushed as she kissed his cheek. "I love that look of surprise on your face. Happens every time I drop by."

"What are you doing here?"

He glanced toward the door to his private quarters, but it was closed.

"Well, I couldn't bear the thought of your gathering dust during the holidays again. I bring gifts and an invitation to dine at my home tomorrow night. Indeed, I have had a bedchamber made ready for you to stay Christmas Eve and spend Christmas Day with us too. Won't that be lovely?"

He hesitated. He had planned to spend the night curled up with Amy in his arms and every night thereafter. However, after Lady Templeton's leave-taking, he was not sure that was possible.

He should not leave Amy alone in the shop until he got to the bottom of this. "You should have written me first before making plans. I am not sure I can make dinner. Tomorrow will be our busiest day, and I had planned a quiet Christmas Day to recuperate."

She frowned severely. "You work too hard. Diana always said you declined so many invitations because you wanted to be alone with her instead. But she is gone, Harpie. You must move on and meet someone who can make you laugh again. Come to luncheon and let me introduce you around."

Harper caught her arm and steered her toward the front door. "I am not unhappy, Thallia. Do not meddle."

"I've invited several lovely young women to join us, widows for the most part, for you to be introduced to and charm. And not one of them frequents your shop, so don't think about declining on the mistaken fear of losing a patron. If they won't do for a wife or lover, they might do for a future customer one day."

He sighed and leaned close. "I always thought your marriage was the worst thing that happened to me. Next thing I know, you'll be having Wayland drag me to some sordid brothel to ease my nonexistent celibacy."

"He could, but then I'd have to kill him for even thinking of such a place." Thallia pivoted. "Wait, what do you mean nonexistent?"

He sighed and signaled to her carriage. The trouble with Thallia was that they had always been far too open about their private affairs. She had been at him for months to take a lover. "Just go home, and I will see you on Christmas Day as we always do."

"Oh, you've met someone? Do tell."

"Enough, Thallia," he said in warning, "or no silken sheets for your bed this Christmas."

"You got them?"

"I cannot believe you doubt me." He helped her into the

carriage and sent her home. He shivered and raced back inside, stamping his feet at the doormat to remove the snow before he tramped it farther inside.

He had to talk to Amy. "Mind the shop, Mr. Hunter. On second thought, close up too."

"Don't mind if I do." Hunter grinned as he looked around with a proprietary air. "Don't mind indeed."

CHAPTER TWELVE

AMY CRINGED as the little door to her housekeeper's room burst open, bathing her in brighter light. That woman had certainly recognized her and revealed her true feelings to Harper. She must also have known what she had become too. She was certain to be thrown out into the cold. And high time too.

Harper held a candle high. "What the devil are you doing in here?"

He sounded angry. "Hiding."

"What from?"

"Everything." Amy scooted off the empty tea chest and faced the man she had come to admire. "I'll go."

"You are not going anywhere until I have an explanation."

Amy shivered. "I don't have a good one. That is the lady who called on my mother. The one who made me wear my Sunday best on a Wednesday and argued with her."

"I could believe that. That particular family is well known for being hard to please." He sighed and held out his arms. "Come here. For a moment there though I thought she might have known what we've done together."

"I've not seen her since well before my mother died." Amy turned aside, although she longed to accept the comfort of his arms. "Can everyone see that I'm a whore just by looking at me?"

"Absolutely not." Harper stepped forward, wrapped his arms around her, and squeezed her tightly. "You're my housekeeper now. It is a respectable position. What you had to do in the past is not something she will ever find out from me."

Amy patted his hand, but her heart was breaking. Lady Templeton could still cause problems. "I wish I had met you sooner."

"Me too." Harper lifted her bodily and carried her out into the warm kitchen. He dropped her on her feet, rested one hand on the tabletop, and peered into her face. "Hunter will close today."

"But sir! The shop."

"The shop can wait." He straightened. "I won't allow you to huddle in a dark room and fear the worst is about to drop on our heads. You have done nothing wrong."

"But I..."

He covered her lips with his fingers. "No more of that."

"You cannot wipe away my past so easily." Her chest tightened. "I sold my body to strangers."

"I wish those other men had never happened to you. That we'd been introduced properly." He teased her jaw with his fingertips. "I would have called to see you the next day, and the next, and if you had liked me enough, I think I would have kept coming back."

A beautiful dream. "If we'd have met like that, I wouldn't know how wicked you are."

"And I would not have known your taste."

"I like the way we met." She would never regret the time she had spent with this man. "You showed me desire and tenderness don't need to be strangers."

Harper had given her hope that someday she might have a place to call her own.

He nodded. "There is so much more we can share, my lovely one. So much, and all of it will make you scream out my name."

Amy had to laugh at his assurance. "Are you sure of that?"

"Absolutely, and I will prove it tonight when we are truly alone together."

"Please," Amy begged, flexing her arms, and gaining no release.

"Not yet," Harper whispered against her quim before kissing her skin lightly. He teased her opening again with his fingers and blew lightly over her sex.

Amy could not take much more of this torture. Harper had kept her at the precipice so long. She needed to feel him. "Now?"

"Patience, my lovely one." His touch slipped upward from her folds and his palm flattened on her stomach. "That reminds me. I wanted to ask how old you are."

"Aging a little bit faster thanks to this torture." She flexed her fingers and wriggled to no avail. Harper had managed to strap her over his sturdy kitchen table very securely indeed. She had satin sheets beneath her body, a soft cushion beneath her head and hips, but still she was his plaything. She did not complain very seriously about his behavior because he did and would make her feel so very good eventually.

He teased her sides and then flicked her nipple. "How old?"

Amy's pussy twitched. "Would you believe sixteen?"

He choked and coughed. "Good God, I hope not. I would feel like a dirty old man in comparison."

"That is not the description I would use. Handsome, distinguished. Wickedly wise for your years," she murmured but then almost laughed as he groaned at her description. It was about time she had some fun at Harper's expense. She had been teased and left wanting for the best part of an hour. Harper kept distracting her with conversation each time her release came within reach. "I am two and twenty years. Very worldly, but obviously not wise enough to have predicted the depths of your depravity and the breadth of your sins."

For all the strangeness of what he was doing to her body, Amy did not want him to stop. She was ready to explode. If he would just touch her clitoris one more time, she would scream.

"The perfect age," he whispered, dropping a kiss to her hip. "My only sin is how badly I want to fuck you. To make you want me just as desperately as I want you," he said, his voice tight.

"I'm yours. Please," she begged as her pussy twitched again. "I don't think I can wait any longer. I'm so close to coming that I will not be able to help myself."

He nipped her inner thigh suddenly, then licked a long stretch of her skin up her thigh. "Is this really so sinful if your body responds so well to what I do?"

He touched her opening, swirled his finger about, but then pressed inside with a dark, desperate groan.

Amy tossed her head, panting from the pleasure of his invasion. "It feels wicked. No one else has asked to do this to me."

"You might be right that I'm wicked," he whispered. He nipped at her thigh, and his breath across her wet skin was rough. "This feels like something only I should do to you. Breathe."

He did something, and the burn and stretch intensified. She arched her back, writing on his fingers, overwhelmed by the pressure building inside her. The tension eased a little as he withdrew slowly. He teased her a little longer with short in and out thrusts of his fingers.

Amy's clitoris pulsed even without him touching her

anywhere, and she knew what that meant. "Oh God, Harper. I can't stop."

His mouth descended on her quim, and he sucked and licked until she was screaming his name, straining at her bonds in a bid to escape the ecstasy consuming her. She panted hard as Harper tore at her fetters and tugged her down the table.

When he pressed inside her, he groaned and set up a furious pace of hard thrusts, probing her depths with wild abandon as he chanted her name. Amy loved the way he wanted to be with her. She loved everything about the handsome shopkeeper, which brought an unforeseen realization.

His fingers dug hard into her hips as he whispered her name reverently.

She had fallen in love with the man.

As he continued to make love to her, moving beyond her sight, her heart expanded and then shrank in sorrow. She had lost her heart to a man who could not possibly love her back in the same fashion. Sex was something they did well together in the privacy of his residence, but outside this secluded world they had no future. The most she could ever be was his lover.

He withdrew and turned her over, so her legs dangled over the table edge. "Brace yourself."

Amy caught hold of the table edge as he surged back inside her body again, taking her hard and fast from behind. Even spent, Amy loved to feel him taking his pleasure. He was so different from the men who paid her for the use of her body.

He'd made her feel special.

He cupped her quim and skimmed her slit, but Amy felt nothing. Nothing but the keen loss of what might have been. She laid her cheek against the soft silk as he tried to inflame her desire and failed.

"Amy?"

"Come, sir. I cannot again tonight."

He groaned as he came, shoved hard enough inside her that the table rattled, and then he fell over her back. Trapped beneath him, Amy tried to bury her feelings. Falling in love was the worst thing she could have done. He still loved his late wife. He could not yet put the woman aside along with her things. Amy was doomed to love alone, and there was not anything she could do about that.

He eased back, and Amy remained splayed on the table, boneless from his pleasures and unwilling to face him and a future of disappointment. Her mother had loved her father, but he had already been married had not cared enough to divorce his wife so Amy might be recognized. Amy had not realized how much that must have hurt her mother.

She was a fool, and she blinked back tears of frustration and hopelessness.

Harper, unaware of her inner turmoil, stroked her spine and then eased her up. "Have I worn you out?"

"A little, perhaps," she whispered, fighting back her emotions. She kept her chin lowered so he would not see her pain as he wrapped a blanket around her shoulders. Oh, she loved the way he treated her, rough and yet so very tenderly afterward. Always making sure she was comfortable and warm, a perfectly wicked gentleman.

He kissed her brow. "Put your arms around my neck and hold on to me."

She expected a kiss but was surprised when he lifted her into his strong arms. "We'd best get into bed. Tomorrow is our busiest day. We'll need our wits about us from first light."

Harper carried her from the kitchen naked, then up the narrow flight of stairs.

Amy had expected to be taken to her own room, which Harper

had allowed her to furnish from his store that evening. Everything was new; she had kept an accounting of her expenditure and had been very frugal. Harper had also insisted she take a few personal items to wear upon her person. She now owned a thick coat, woolen stockings, and a new navy-blue day gown and soft white chemise. She had planned to admire each and every item before blowing out the candle.

"I like your side of the bed for sleeping," she whispered quickly, hoping not to see any of Mrs. Cabot's things before she closed her eyes that night. The sight would surely break her heart after her discovery of having fallen in love.

Harper smiled and gently deposited her in his hastily repaired bed, tucking her into his side firmly. He pressed a long kiss to her brow before drawing back. "I'll remove the evidence of our tryst downstairs and return soon."

As soon as he was gone from the room, Amy buried her face in her pillow and cried her eyes out.

CHAPTER THIRTEEN

HARPER GLANCED UP SOURLY, then took one long step to the side. Someone had hung mistletoe near the sales counter, and he was not happy to see it over his head and a customer eyeing him with barely concealed expectation. He did not kiss indiscriminately. He only wanted to kiss Amy in fact. He'd had one near miss with a customer so far that day, but he had quickly feigned ignorance, leaving a disappointed lady lagging behind as he hurried away.

The door to his apartment opened, and Amy swept in from the kitchen carrying a fresh coffeepot. The gentlemen in the window chairs were polite to her, and he was pleased that none noticed how pretty and fresh she was. She was wearing the new blue gown he'd given her, that he'd taken great delight in dressing her in himself that morning after making love, acting as lady's maid between decadent kisses. The color brought out the warmth of her skin. Watching her made his heart skip a beat.

"I see the new housekeeper has settled in well," Hunter murmured as he ambled over.

"Yes, I think so."

Amy, finished with her task, retreated to the kitchen where he knew she would prefer to remain during the workday.

Hunter eyed the connecting door. "What was that business with Lady Templeton about yesterday? She never fainted when she first saw Pelaw."

"Apparently the countess had a past acquaintance with Amy's mother, who was a dressmaker before her death." He swallowed, hoping revealing so much was in Amy's best interests. "I think there must have been bad blood between the women."

"I see." Hunter polished his glasses. "I'm curious, who is Miss Mellish's father? She has never mentioned the man once that I recall. Is he dead or just absent?"

Amy had not mentioned a father because she did not know his name. A not so uncommon occurrence and probably best not spoken of by his staff. However, he suddenly recalled the countess's fury at finding Amy here. The wealthy often sought comfort outside their marriages. Lady Templeton might know of Amy's irregular birth and had taken offense at having tea served to her by someone born out of wedlock. It was hardly Amy's fault that her father acted without honor and hadn't married her mother. He should have if he'd any honor in his soul... unless he was already married to someone else.

His heart took a strange turn as he came to the most uncomfortable conclusion. Amy's father had been married, and Lady Templeton might know exactly who he was because the connection could be a little too close to home.

He cursed softly, but Hunter heard.

"That's what I thought it might be too," Hunter murmured sadly. "Miss Mellish does remind me of another of our customers."

"What? Who?"

"One related very closely to the countess."

Amy's father might be one of the Ford devils. He rubbed his brow. "Hell."

"Exactly. This could mean trouble for us." Hunter turned his back to the shop and slouched against the counter. "There are two things you could do, but either way you are going to lose."

If Amy was related to a member of Lady Templeton's family, there would indeed be many problems he did not want to think about. "What do you believe my choices are?"

"Give up your housekeeper or prepare to lose the entire Ford family account." Hunter sighed. "You cannot keep both. It's all up to you, unfortunately."

Amy returned, tea tray balanced carefully between her hands. She approached them, smiling softly, a perfect example of decorum and grace. "Something to warm you both."

She slid the tray onto the table and set out two cups.

"Thank you, Amy," Harper said as Hunter replied in much the same tone.

The other man took the first sip as Amy hurried away. He grunted and sipped his tea again. "I thought I knew which I'd choose a moment ago, but the woman does have her merits."

Harper sipped from his cup, noting that Amy had added brandy to the mix without asking if they would prefer it. Of course, they both would have said yes if asked. Hunter kept a flask under the sales counter usually, but with so many customers that day, they had not tried to slip any into previous cups of tea.

A warm glow filled his chest, and not just from the effect of the brandy. "Quite thoughtful of her," he murmured softly.

The Ford account was worth nearly a thousand pounds a year, sometimes more, not to mention the complement of their referrals to friends within the *ton*. He had a lot to lose.

He finished his tea, reinforced for an afternoon of brisk activity. Despite her kindness, in the end Hunter would choose the money over Amy. However, in the past year Harper had learned a painful truth. Money did not matter if you hadn't anyone to share it with.

He liked Amy very much. Enough that he could almost accept the loss of the Ford account with only a trace of regret. Enough that he wanted to keep her around for as long as possible. A long time. As much as his remaining years perhaps.

He set his hand to the tabletop as he imagined any sort of future with her. He wanted Amy desperately, and the best thing to do was marry her to ensure she would always be safe and respected. Always protected and warm.

Could he give his heart so completely to a woman he barely knew?

A woman gasped, and Harper glanced toward the sound.

A customer had Amy trapped between his hands and was kissing her under another hung branch of mistletoe!

His blood boiled, and Hunter's hand dropped onto his shoulder and held him in place before he could rush to her defense. "Steady. It is just a mistletoe kiss. Don't make a scene."

However, every customer in the shop was watching a kiss that went on too long. The gentlemen by the window came to their feet; their wives begin to whisper and point.

Amy broke free, putting distance between herself and the man. She cradled her wrist, and her eyes were wild. "Sir, you should be ashamed of yourself."

Harper broke free of Hunter's restraining hand and rushed toward her. "What is going on?"

"Oh, don't be too harsh on her, Cabot," the man said as he grinned, leering at Amy. "You have a lovely shop. Very welcoming, and the staff are delightful."

He glanced into Amy's pale face and saw her bottom lip tremble.

"We won't be so welcoming in the future," Harper warned. "You will apologize and get out."

The fellow appeared shocked. "What?"

"You heard me," he said quietly. "She is under my protection. I will not have my staff harassed by any of my customers. Is that understood?"

"It's all right, Mr. Cabot." Amy grasped his arm but then winced and rubbed her wrist. "It was just a misunderstanding."

"Was it?"

"Harper!" his sister Thallia called out, making him cringe. "Darling, do you ever notice your poor baby sister when she arrives to visit? And I brought my husband along too."

A few customers laughed outright, but Harper rolled his eyes. "This isn't a good time, Thallia."

"On the contrary. My timing is always excellent." She smiled sweetly and squeezed between him and Miss Mellish. "You are just the dear I've been looking for, Miss Mellish."

"I am?"

"Indeed. I've had a terrible accident with my coat, and I am in need of your assistance." Thallia waved her hand. "Do be a dear, Harpie, and tend the store while Miss Mellish assists me."

His brother by marriage, George Wayland, shrugged. "She always gets what she wants, and you know it."

Harper shook his head as Amy was pulled away from him and toward the back room. A piece of him went too, but he was afraid of what harm Thallia might do to his situation with Amy. He did not want Amy scared off before he had had a chance to decide what he wanted for the rest of his life.

He scowled at his brother by marriage. "I had such hopes that you might one day have some influence with her."

His brother-in-law eased closer and dropped his voice low.

"My influence is absolute in matters best kept to the bedchamber. Now, I hear there is good coffee to be had."

He pointed him toward the fresh pot. "Help yourself."

Harper glanced around but noted the fellow who had kissed Amy had fled the shop while his sister had claimed his attention. He strolled to the sales counter. "Find out who that man was and make sure he and his lot never step across our threshold again."

"A Mr. Young of Old Compton Street. He has an older sister who comes in alone on Fridays. Seems a shame to punish her too." Hunter frowned. "So, you've decided on her then?"

"I've no idea what you mean."

"I'll keep your secret if you're not ready to bend the knee yet, but she's good for you."

And he intended to be very good for her, and not just in the bedroom. Sex before breakfast had always been his secret love. Wild sex for no reason at all but that he wanted Amy was the greatest aphrodisiac he knew. Keeping her from the clutches of lewd men ranked very high on his list. To do that he had best marry her and make sure she was properly protected by his name.

However, a man did not marry lightly. Not at his age. He was rich and should seek the counsel of his solicitor first. He was still on good terms with his late wife's family too, seeing them daily. He would not like that to change. They might take his remarriage hard.

Thallia and her husband, however, seemed pleased enough to meet Amy, having saved her from the scene he had been about to make with Mr. Young. He sighed. He was in for a challenging time ahead.

It was Christmas Eve, and if he intended to marry Amy, his timing could not be worse. Tomorrow, Christmas Day, was also the anniversary of his wife's death—a date that was cemented in his memory as his greatest failure.

CHAPTER FOURTEEN

AMY WOKE long after the sun had risen. She remained still, listening to the distant sounds of London muted by the walls of the haberdashery, listening to Harper's steady breaths at her side.

She should turn to him and discover if he was awake and desirous as he usually was at this hour of the day. But she stayed still, content in the moment of near-perfect peace.

She had never expected to feel so happy the day she had paused outside Harper's busy shop. Her luck had changed that day, and so much for the better.

She turned her head, only to discover Harper was sitting on the edge of it already. Judging by the shirt and waistcoat he was wearing, he had been awake for some time and ready to face the world. His back was to her, so she could not see his expression. His shoulders shook, and he wiped his face the next moment.

Was he crying?

Amy froze as Harper stretched toward a table and picked up a glove that had once belonged to his wife. Unwilling to interrupt so private a moment, Amy lowered her lids until she could barely see and pretended to still be sleeping. He ran the glove between his fingers, staring off into space, and then held it to his nose. He breathed deep, then sighed, and returned the glove exactly to where it had once lain.

Knowing he was thinking of *her* broke her heart.

He leaned forward and braced his forearms on his thighs, held up his hand to the morning light. In his fingers was a pretty ring, a delicate pearl surrounded by gold. He tucked it into his waistcoat pocket.

He turned suddenly, catching her watching him. "Ah, good morning."

Amy stretched, pretending to be just waking, but her thoughts were still on the ring he had pocketed. "Good morning, Harper. What time is it?"

He slumped back onto the bed and came to rest with his head on her thigh. "Nearing the time I must go to visit my sister."

"So late? Oh, I'm so sorry I slept so long."

"Don't be sorry. I'd much rather have watched you sleep than wake you with my selfishness."

"What selfishness?"

He captured her hand and kissed the back of it, then brushed her fingers against his lips. "We have been keeping very late hours. Very vigorous hours in this bed, too. You needed time to rest."

Amy blushed. "Happy hours spent in your arms. I cannot be sorry for the time we have spent together."

Harper dropped her hand.

Her words had no positive effect on his mood, and the silence grew heavy between them. His lack of response troubled her. Usually, he was very quick to insist he had been satisfied by their trysts.

Amy glanced away, heart twisting with fear, only to notice the late Mrs. Cabot's gloves where they waited. She closed her eyes as her heart lurched. He missed his wife so much. So much that he would never notice how she hung on his every word.

Harper kept his silence, and she feared she knew why. The words she'd uttered, her soul-deep conviction that the best thing in her life was the day they'd met, was likely his lowest moment as a gentleman.

He was a good and decent man, and he was keeping a scandalous woman as his mistress. He must feel shame for that.

She wished Lady Templeton had never come to remind Harper he dallied with a fallen woman. He had not taken the confrontation well, and she was afraid that his altercation with the customer who had stolen a kiss beneath the mistletoe had made him regret the bargain they had struck even more. She had not enjoyed the kiss from the stranger. If not for Harper's sister's timely arrival, she dreaded to think of the scene that might have unfolded.

He must be feeling guilt over having her in his bed, a fallen woman lying where a good woman had once belonged.

Amy had no place in his world, but she had nowhere else to go.

Convinced he was regretting their arrangement, Amy drank in Harper's profile, his straight nose, his generous lips that could muddle her mind with the slightest brush. He had closed his eyes, but she recalled the color with perfect clarity. Golden brown, like the earth of a freshly plowed Brentwood field. She did not miss the place, but she would miss Harper when he tired of her.

She sucked in a shaky breath, wondering if that moment had already come and gone.

Amy ran her fingers through his hair, toying with the soft dark strands while she could. "You should go. You promised Mrs. Wayland not to be late."

He sat up. "You'll be all right?"

"I'll be very comfortable on my own."

He stood and tugged down his waistcoat and then reached for a package he had left near the bed. He showed it to her. "My sister's gift, imported silk sheets for her husband's bed. I have a friend who conducts trade with India merchants. It's a surprise for her husband."

"I'm certain he'll love the gift. They both will."

Harper checked his pockets as he drew close. "One kiss before I go, and no more than that or I might never leave."

She stretched up and planted her lips against his. Harper cupped her cheek and kissed her with a lazy ease that spoke of familiarity. She clung to his arm a moment, then released him. Her cheeks were hot, and her eyes stung as he collected his coat and hat with a cheery wave and departed without looking back.

Amy waited in bed until his footsteps faded and the sound of a door closing echoed through the empty building. She brought her knees to her chest and released a shaky breath. What should she do?

Should she go before longing for his love brought her undone? It seemed the best course of action, but not an easy one for her. She slipped out of bed, her legs unsteady in the face of what she needed to do, and removed her own gown from where she had stored it beneath the bed. In the time she had been here, she had managed to launder the garment and carry out repairs. Her gown was faded and worn in places, but it was hers.

She stripped off her nightgown and folded it carefully while she shivered. Harper had given her a chemise when her own had fallen apart, and she threw that over her head before she became thoroughly frozen. She stroked her upper thighs through the soft fabric, remembering how many times Harper had delighted in removing the garment from her body. What he had done after made her long for him to never stop.

She shook her head sadly. At this rate, she would never do what needed to be done.

She slipped on her own gown, but as she was buttoning it up the fabric and stitches began to tear around her shoulders. She rushed to the mirror, eyes widening as she twisted to see it continue to fall apart before her eyes. Her own gown was so unwearable it would not even do for kitchen rags.

She bit her lip. She had to wear something when she left, and with no other choice Amy slipped on the lovely navy-blue gown she had worn yesterday. The fit was perfect, and her eyes filled with tears.

She would always remember how tenderly Harper had dressed and undressed her yesterday as if she belonged to him.

When she was finally ready, Amy did not dare look back. She hurried downstairs, collected her hat and coat. As she put her arm in the sleeve, the rear door rattled with the force of a knock.

She stared at it. Harper had promised no one was expected today.

"I say, Miss Mellish, please open the door," a male voice said. "Lady Templeton urgently requests a word with you."

The countess had come back!

She backed away as the knocking resumed. She could always leave by the front door, but then Harper's neighbors might see her, and she could not lock it behind her. Her only way out was through the rear door. Amy eased to the door, listening carefully to the silence beyond. Another knock sounded and she jumped. She was unprepared to face the woman today and hear of her wickedness. She pressed her lips together and wondered how long she might have to wait before she went away.

"We know you are in there. There is something that must be said. It is vitally important that you open the door at once."

Amy was torn, but she had been brought up to respect the nobility no matter her feelings or how rude the request. What harm could it do to hear the woman out? It was Christmas Day. "I'm coming."

She threw back the bolts and opened the door. Behind the grooms, a small glossy black carriage waited in the filthy lane. One groom rushed to open the carriage door, and the countess descended, bundled up to her nose in furs and a heavy wool cloak.

The countess hurried inside, shut the door on her servants, and glanced around. "Ah, alone at last."

"My lady. What a surprise to see you here."

"Indeed, I should be in Essex with my daughters, enjoying the holiday, but needs must and here I am."

Amy frowned at that. "How may I be of assistance? Are you in need of an item from the shop? Mr. Cabot is with his family for Christmas Day, but I could help you I think."

"No." She set her fur muffler aside. "I'm here for you and only you."

"Why?" Amy drew back. "You can only disapprove of me."

The countess stared at her hard but then shook her head. "That is simply not true. But I will say again that you do not belong here."

Amy straightened her spine. "Then where do I belong?"

Lady Templeton frowned at her tone. "Somewhere better than a shop or in the kitchen of one. Do you believe you were meant for better things than being a housekeeper?"

Amy shrugged. "I have nothing better."

"Then let me help you find your way out of this drudgery."

"I am not a drudge. I love working for Mr. Cabot." She did not mention she loved Mr. Cabot too. The countess would never approve of a servant longing for her employer. She turned away to make tea for the countess.

The countess seated herself at the table and set her hands in her lap, watching her very closely. "Your mother was never very gracious about accepting help either, and your father... well, let us not speak of his carelessness. I have a home ready for you, servants employed to see to your every need. When you are settled and ready, we can talk about what else you might want from life."

Her curiosity piqued at the mention of her father. This lady knew who he was. Amy was sure of it. She was also sure the woman did not approve of him very much. However, she would never get answers if she demanded them. She would have to lead the countess along a little more. She set tea and the best China before the countess then poured for her. "What else is there in life?"

"Marriage, babies. Love. You are very pretty, and many a man would find you a worthy bride."

"I am humbled that you want to help me." Amy licked her lips, glancing down at her hands. She wanted to be honest and see if the countess's offer stood. If not, she was no worse off than she was now. "I am ruined, my lady. Beyond question. I don't think I would make anyone an acceptable wife."

Lady Templeton's cup rattled into its saucer. "And that is my failing too."

Amy looked up, startled to find the countess with tears in her eyes. "No matter what has transpired, child, the offer stands. It is our way to look after family, no matter how unpleasant the situation might be. You should have come to me or sent word of your mother's death."

"Family?" Amy frowned. "I don't understand. My mother had no living relatives."

The countess grimaced. "My husband was not a careful man, child. He made mistakes that you are now paying for."

Amy paled. Did she understand properly? Was Lady Templeton suggesting she was the offspring of Lord Templeton?

An earl. That would explain so much of her mother's hostility to the countess's monthly visits.

The countess squirmed under her scrutiny. Amy's heart pounded. "Oh, my stars. I am sorry. I had no idea who my father was."

"I see that now." The countess shook her head. "You will allow me to take care of you."

It was not a question. The countess would probably hound her until she agreed. She remembered the way the countess and her mother had talked together. Amy was not likely to hold out for long in the face of her usual persistence. A rich and powerful woman wanted to make up for the mistake, her birth, had caused her. It was quite a shock to Amy. She could not imagine how upsetting this must be for the countess, and she had known all along. Had she patronized her mother's services as a dressmaker simply as a means to keep an eye on Amy?

She might have. Amy sank into a chair at the table and rubbed her hand over the well-used surface. She could accept the countess's help. She needed that help. Her only regret was leaving Harper. "I would be very grateful for your assistance, my lady."

The countess sighed. "Collect your things, and I'll deliver you to your new home now."

"Now?"

"Yes, now. Once you are settled, I need to return to Newberry Park." She sighed again. "And surely you would not want to stay another day as a mere servant when you could have the comfort of your own bed and hearth."

"Yes, of course." She was not really a servant; she was a kept woman and had been content that way until this morning. Amy glanced around a little sadly. She had been very happy here, but she had always known she could not stay. Harper would always love Diana Cabot. She could not possibly compete with a love that spanned death. "I should write Mr. Cabot a note to explain where I've gone. He has been so good to me and worried that the murderer has not been caught. I would not like him to fear for my safety upon his return."

"The murderer plaguing Bond Street was caught days ago and sent to trial I'm told. It has been in all the papers, so there is no reason to worry unnecessarily. You'll be far from any unpleasantness in Mayfair."

"He never told me," Amy whispered in shock. Harper had omitted to mention the danger had passed. Had he done it so she would accept the position with him and stay in his bed?

She was furious only a moment and then softened. What harm had his deception really done her? He had kept her warm by lighting every fireplace. Kept her in his own bed, fed her with his own fingers sometimes too. Doing everything in his power to make her feel cared for. Making her fall in love with him.

She took a breath, loving him still. "I can be ready to go the moment my letter is done."

She smiled brightly, fighting back tears. She would not change anything about their time together. Because of him, she had recovered her faith in human kindness. She would miss him dreadfully, but it was for the best.

"Well, in any case your new servants will be there to protect you or face my considerable wrath. Your new drawing room will be a considerable improvement on this chamber. I have had all the seasonal trimmings of a Christmas set up, so you won't feel lonely there."

"I was happy here." She was sure she had made Harper happy too, at least for a little while.

"Mr. Cabot will find a replacement soon enough," Lady Templeton said.

That he might well do. If Harper returned her affection, she would see him again one day. Her heart filled with unstoppable hope that this might not be the end of their affair. If he possessed any deeper feelings for her, he would come to call on her if he knew where to find her.

Amy quickly penned an explanation to Mr. Cabot for her departure and left the folded note on the table so he would see it when he returned. She wished him well and then added one last line, expressing a hope that perhaps he might consider calling on her one day. She hoped she did not sound too needy. She did not tell him she loved him or that her heart was breaking at the very thought of never seeing him again.

But if he truly cared anything for her, he would pay a call for the express purpose of ensuring she was content with her new situation.

After that, Amy wanted nothing more than to kiss him one last time to end their Christmas affair.

CHAPTER FIFTEEN

AS MISS WILSON shifted back toward her mother, Harper breathed a sigh of relief. It was Christmas Day, a most uncomfortable time of year for him because it brought forth so many regrets and memories. It was a celebration without his wife. An end of a year with only his guilt for company.

He glanced about those gathered, friends he had shunned since Diana's death, and felt a pang of remorse for his past behavior. He had abandoned these good people and wallowed in self-pity for far too long. However, the machinations of those determined to cheer him out of his mopes was painfully obvious and very futile. His friends meant well by pushing Miss Wilson into conversation with him, but he had already decided to remarry.

This afternoon, when he returned home, he would pack Diana's things and give them all away. Most would return to her family if they wanted them, the rest he would pass to servants in his sister's home.

It was time to put the past away and think about his future.

A future with the delicious Amy Mellish sharing his bed.

He intended to go down on bended knee tonight, after leaving here, and ask for her hand in marriage with every argument for the match at his disposal.

He didn't care about the circumstances of her birth, lack of society connections, or the possibility of future difficulty with Lady Templeton should she be displeased.

He cared only about Amy.

So often he had found it hard to sit through this interminable Christmas luncheon and keep smiling in the face of everyone's concern without giving himself away. He wished he could have brought Amy with him, to have her sit by his side in this warm and cozy room and be entertained by the lively conversation of good people he wanted her to come to know.

Leaving her behind at home had been necessary, but he could not help but feel now that he had been mistaken in parting with her today. However, crying off from his sister's luncheon would have been inexcusably rude.

Thallia patted his hand, drawing his attention. "Would it hurt you to be a little friendlier to Miss Wilson? You've hardly spoken more than a few words, and she's very shy as it is."

"I don't want to lead anyone to misunderstand," he murmured. He knew Thallia meant well, but he wished she would drop the matter. "Stop pushing me into conversation with young women in want of a husband, and I will be very talkative indeed."

"I doubt you understand how to be agreeable to any woman." Thallia huffed. "Harper, your poor wife hardly knew you cared for her right up until the moment you proposed. You are not exactly the easiest of men to love. Out there, some poor girl is probably pining for your smiles, and you would not even know until you saw her tears with your own eyes."

"She couldn't be crying."

Thallia frowned severely. "Why not? Do you think you are unworthy of a second love?"

It was probably a good time to hint to his sister that he was going to marry Amy if she agreed. "Because we've known each other for only a short period of time."

Thallia's eyebrows shot up. "So, there is a woman responsible for that faraway look in your eyes and your silence today?"

"Yes," he admitted, watching her reaction carefully. "She is someone who has become very important to me."

"Then I'd like to shake her hand." Thallia sat back, grinning to the occupants scattered around the room. "Ladies and gentlemen, it seems my poor widowed brother isn't as sad as I first feared. His head has been turned by a very fine lady indeed. There is a match to be made very soon."

A collective sigh swept through the room. Miss Wilson clapped her hands together, beaming at the news.

"Thallia," Harper warned, worried that they would get too far ahead in their congratulations than necessary. "She has no idea of my plans for us."

Thallia merely waved aside his protest. "You are among friends, dear brother. We all admire you and want you to be happy. If that is already the case, then our wishes have been granted. It is the best Christmas wish to have been delivered. I am sure she will accept you."

He glanced about him, noticing smiles of agreement. His was filled with discomfort and could even feel a blush coloring his cheeks. "She hasn't said yes yet. I haven't even asked."

Wayland brought him a drink. "But you will."

"When the time is right, and she will agree," Thallia continued, smiling warmly at her own husband. She patted his hand again. "Nothing short of love could distract you from talking about your shop from morning till night. You have hardly spoken of the Christmas Eve rush for the first time in years. That is why we were so concerned by your silence. We feared you were still pining for

Diana's loss, but this new preoccupation bodes very well for the future."

"Why her? What sort of woman is she?" Mrs. Wilson asked with a smile.

The reasons he had fallen for Amy were difficult to put into words. "Kind, very thoughtful."

"And her family?" Wayland asked. "Are they prominent?"

"She has no one. Her mother died a year ago." He nodded, warming to the topic. However, editing out the past year of Amy's life would be essential. The less he said now, the easier it would be for Amy to shape her own past in conversation with these people later. "We met again recently, and I discovered she and her mother share a connection with me through a mutual customer. Her mother was a seamstress, and quite good I understand."

Thallia smiled. "And you are just the sort of man to understand that a lady must have exactly the right embellishments on her gowns. I am so pleased and look forward to meeting her."

They had already met, but he would not mention that in mixed company. He would pull Thallia and her husband aside before he left and ask that they overlook the first time and situation when they'd met Amy. "I will arrange it at the first opportunity."

"Excellent." His brother-in-law enthused. "We will host a dinner in her honor and toast your upcoming wedding over some of my best champagne."

Advice for the dinner and wedding flowed nonstop around them for a full ten minutes, then another topic was seized upon, and he ceased to be the center of attention.

He leaned toward Thallia. "I have to get back to my shop."

"So soon?"

He set his glass aside, keen to return to Amy and propose. It was time to move ahead with his life. "Now I have decided to marry, I have some personal things to take care of."

"Such as?"

"I must pack away Diana's things," he admitted quietly. That morning he had said goodbye to Diana. He had been surprised Amy had not commented on his tears. It was a shock he'd had any left to weep after so much time had passed since her death. It was time to get on with living his life to the fullest. He stood and said his goodbyes to everyone.

Thallia followed him into the relative privacy of the entrance hall.

"Oh Harper," Thallia scolded, grabbing his hand, and squeezing. "Why have you not packed Diana's things away yet?"

"I couldn't." He settled his hat on his head. "I left everything just as it was that last day."

"Then it is beyond time to clean house." Thallia brushed his shoulder soothingly. "If your new love were to discover Diana's belongings are still around, she might have second thoughts about the depths of your devotion to her. You cannot let her know of it before you propose. She might feel strange knowing you'd removed them so soon after meeting her."

He thought of Amy in his room, in his bed. She would have seen Diana's things when she used the dresser in the mornings and at night.

A sudden discomfort seized him. How much time had she spent in his bedroom outside of the time they were making love? He had always found her in the kitchen. Had she used the dresser mirror even once?

His breath caught, realizing that Amy could have been very uncomfortable in that room and not spoken of it. Had she asked to sleep on his side of the bed so she would be far away from the reminders left behind by another woman?

He closed his eyes at his blindness. "She knows."

"Well, if she is still speaking to you, then you are in luck. She must love you to put up with such a slight."

He tugged on his waistcoat, smoothing it in his impatience. "I am such a fool. I have to go home."

"Good. Dispense with the past and embrace the future. Diana would understand. She would not have wanted you to be alone forever."

"I hope so."

"Now, with all possible haste, dear brother, go and see this woman of yours." She pushed at his shoulder. "Pledge your heart to your lady and let me know how soon I can plan the wedding breakfast."

He raked his hands through his hair, worried that Thallia was going to be disappointed in him. "Don't make any plans yet. My love is already living in my home and knows about Diana's things. I may have some apologies to make before any wedding can be agreed upon."

Thallia's eyes widened. "The new housekeeper?"

He nodded. "The very one, and I do not deserve her."

"No, you don't." Thallia rolled her eyes. "But a proposal of marriage today might just make up for your lack of insight into the female mind."

"I hope so." Harper kissed his sister good-bye and then rushed out the door, striding into falling snow with the very great fear now that Amy might not have a clue she had claimed his heart completely.

CHAPTER SIXTEEN

AFTER A FEW HOURS alone in her new home, Amy was convinced that another woman had caught Mr. Cabot's eye at his sister's Christmas luncheon, and he had not come home to see her letter. Amy had explored her new home from top to bottom. She had chosen a pretty chamber for herself and found a French novel in the library. She was finally getting the hang of the language again as the door knocker sounded.

She stood, heart beating wildly, as a servant fled toward the sound and spoke quietly to whoever had come.

The butler returned carrying a small silver tray. "Miss Mellish, I am afraid you have a caller who will not be turned away."

There was a card on the tray, and she picked it up quickly. Mr. Harper Cabot.

She struggled to contain her happiness. "Please, show him in."

The butler frowned. "Shall I call for the housekeeper?"

"That will not be necessary." She trembled anew. If the housekeeper came, Harper would not be able to speak freely. "Mr. Cabot is a friend of my late mother's and completely honorable."

Although the man clearly disapproved, he paced out of the

room and led Harper to her a few moments later. He went away but kept the doors open.

"Miss Mellish," Harper murmured, eyes keen on her person, then quickly scanning the room. "It has been too long."

Amy held out her hand. "An age, sir."

Harper took her fingers in his and squeezed them tightly. "An eternity. I was very pleased to receive your note and new direction," he said softly.

She gestured to a position beside her on the chaise. "I had hoped you might have an interest. May I enquire after your sister? I trust you left her in good health today."

Harper checked the doors. "She is furious with me, but not for leaving her party so early."

Her smile faded. "Did you not enjoy the luncheon and conversation?"

Harper smiled. "The food was, as always, excellent, but the company lacked that which might make my heart lighter."

Amy sighed. "You missed your wife."

"I did, especially so today," he murmured. "My wife passed away exactly one year ago this morning, and everyone at luncheon spoke of her fondly."

That explained his tears as he'd sat on the side of the bed, playing with a dead woman's glove. "I didn't realize the significance of this morning. I am sorry."

"Thank you." He smiled. "I think you would have enjoyed the affair far more than I did. There was an abundance of food and music too. I left early to be with you only to discover you gone. Finding you again has eased my heart."

He'd only come to assure himself that she was happy. "I am safe and well as you see."

"Amy, we need to talk about the future." He caught her hands in his. "There is something I'd like to give you, but there is something I'd like to tell you first."

"Anything."

"I'm a terrible man, careless of my effect on others. I have a tendency to blunder into situations and assume those around me understand what I feel." He smoothed his thumbs over her knuckles. "I have asked so much of you and assumed wrongly that what I felt, you felt too."

"I don't understand. Have I done something to displease you?"

"Quite the contrary. Amy, I admire you very greatly. Despite your desperate situation, you somehow managed to keep that sweetness and light in your soul. And yet there is such strength of character in you too. That night when I discovered you inside that makeshift hovel, I was astounded by your unflinching composure in the presence of a stranger. Anyone else in such desperate straits might have burst into tears or looked for the first opportunity to better their purse." He caressed her cheek. "Not you. You made me a fortune instead with your clever ideas, and I am beyond thankful to have met you."

She squirmed. "I am glad to have been any help."

"I want to give you something that cannot be returned or sold, or traded for something else." He clenched her hands tightly. "I give you my heart, Amy Mellish. Utterly and completely. I have fallen in love with you, and time and distance will not alter that fact."

Her breath caught and her eyes filled with tears at the discovery. "You love me?"

"I do. I will devote myself to keeping you warm, to keeping you safe, and with the best roof over your head that it is possible to give if only you might love me in return."

"I do love you." Amy blinked back tears. "I love you so much it hurts when you're out of sight."

"I want to offer you my name." Harper pulled her into his arms and held her tightly. "Is there truly no one I should ask for your hand in marriage?"

She drew back and dabbed at her eyes. "I could live a life of sin just to see you every day. You don't have to offer for me."

"A marriage or nothing," he insisted, taking her face in his hand, and staring deep into her eyes. "I would be proud to have your arm wrapped around mine. Besides, my sister wants to meet you as soon as possible, and she will insist we wed properly."

"What about those other ladies you met with at luncheon? Your sister had planned an end to your widower status. Would she not be happier if you married one of them? Someone with a purer past?"

"Can you imagine me married to anyone but you? Making love to anyone but you?"

"I would not like that," she whispered through fresh tears. "I only want you to touch me."

"Good." He caressed her face tenderly. "I could have throttled Mr. Young for that mistletoe prank yesterday. I've never felt so unhinged by jealousy in my entire life."

"He surprised me, I swear. I never wanted to kiss that man or to kiss anyone else. Not again."

"I will not allow anyone else to press his bare lips to yours ever again. Even if there is mistletoe hanging about."

"Oh sir, look up," she whispered. "I think you will not disapprove if you were the one to take advantage of me."

His eyes widened at the mistletoe draped from every possible location in the room. "My word, I like the way you think, darling."

She blushed at the endearment and held the feeling of belonging close to her heart. "I hope so."

He caught her against him and kissed her hard. He pressed her gently into the back of the chaise and teased his tongue between her lips, setting her body thrumming with desire. There was a very comfortable bed upstairs in her room, and although she should not tarnish her reputation, she could not help but think she and Harper should share it to celebrate their upcoming marriage.

When he let her up for air, she was breathless.

He pressed his brow to hers. "The shop will be closed an extra day tomorrow and we will, together, decide our happy future if you will invite me back to call on you again."

"Stay the night."

His nostrils flared and then a smile burst from his lips. "I've been a bad influence on you, and I love it. I love you."

She drew back, a grin tugging her lips. Oh, this man made her world so right again. "A good influence if it means we are naked."

"Only when we are alone together."

The drawing room doors snapped shut. "Now this is the most interesting conversation I've ever had the pleasure of interrupting. It is not every day a man walks into the planning of a tryst," a stranger mused, tossing his hat across the room as if he owned it, and bowed. "Viscount Maitland, at your service."

Amy blinked at the dark-haired giant who had invaded her sitting room. "Who are you?"

He slouched a little, and all of a sudden, he seemed far less intimidating. "Ah, I see Mother didn't mention I was coming."

"And your mother is?"

"Lady Templeton."

"Oh. Oh." Amy stepped forward and curtsied to her half-brother, although her cheeks were likely flaming with her embarrassment. "You're Quinn. I mean Lord Maitland. Oh, I never expected to meet you."

"I'm sure you didn't." He glanced around, studying at the abundance of mistletoe with a worried expression, then shook his head. "However, you will find that Fords do not behave as expected, and I like to set the tone for the rest of my siblings when it comes to impropriety. I am fairly certain the others will present themselves in due course."

"Really?"

The viscount nodded, then spared a glance for Harper at last. "And you, sir, I don't believe I caught your name."

"Mr. Harper Cabot of Cabot's Haberdashery. My establishment is on Bond Street."

"I know of it." The viscount pursed his lips a moment. "And the reason you were kissing the lady?"

"Miss Mellish had just agreed to become my wife."

"I see." He tipped his head to look down upon her. "Is this what you'd prefer instead of my mother's meddling?"

Amy nodded, clinging to Harper's arm. "Very much so."

Maitland slapped his gloves across his palm. "Capital. I see I am just in time. Let us negotiate a deal tonight and have the ink dry on the contract. Mother is bound for Essex tomorrow and intends to return to torment you within a fortnight. I must warn you that Mother is already making plans you don't want to know about."

Harper's arm curled around her chest. "Amy? Why does this gentleman think he can speak for you?"

"Oh dear." She winced. How to explain what had never been voiced aloud, and with her father's legitimate son standing in the room. What a pickle.

"Perhaps you would prefer to discuss the nature of our connection in private," the viscount suggested. "I will see if there is paper and such in the library for a marriage contract."

"Thank you."

Harper spun her around to face him. "Why did you really leave with the countess?"

Amy winced again. "Apparently, I am not quite so without family as I had believed."

His eyebrows rose. "Explain."

"I am the illegitimate issue of Lord Templeton. Lord Maitland might have been my elder brother had I not been born a bastard. Not that I wish for Lady Templeton's demise," she said quickly in case Lord Maitland was listening still. She took a deep breath. "The countess has known of my existence all my life; that is why she came to call on my mother so often when I was a girl."

"To glare at your mother?"

"To force her to accept help. You see, Lady Templeton married my father long before he met my mother, and I was conceived. She was unhappy with her husband then, I think she still may be, but she wanted to look after me regardless. Family means a great deal to her, even when it is not legitimate."

He set his hands to his hips. "Then where was she for you this past year? Running in and out of my shop, spending a fortune on everyone but you."

"You must not blame her." Amy wrung her hands. "As I believe I mentioned, I never knew who my father was. Mother never told me his name. I had no idea who she was to me, and Lady Templeton assumed I had always known the purpose of her visits." She sighed. "She did not know my mother had died, or that I had run away, until her next monthly visit, but by then I was long gone. She looked for me for months and months. Discovering me in London and keeping house for you came as a shock. She'd thought me utterly lost since I'd left with nothing but a few shillings to my name."

"And her threats against us?"

Amy grasped his arm. "She wishes to avoid the scandal my relationship to the family would bring, and I can understand her fears. Please forgive her for that. She did not understand that you were not a threat and that you had been so very good to me. She understands better now."

Harper glanced around, eyes narrowing on the comfortable chairs. He frowned. "Well, you seem to have fallen into a very good situation."

"I would have been happy with my little housekeeper's room and a fire."

He sighed. "Seeing you like this has made me realize that my offer of marriage may be less than you deserve."

"No, it isn't." Amy panicked at the idea he was having second thoughts. "I wish only for a roof over my head and you beside me."

"A house. I have funds enough for a proper home for us to live in."

"But you love the shop. I would not have you give it up for me."

"I won't give it up entirely. Hunter has been hinting at becoming a partner this past year, and I think it is time to put my life, and a family, first. Hunter can take over the apartment and more of the responsibilities. You, my lovely one, can have anything your heart desires."

The viscount coughed as he poked his head through the door. "All done discussing our troublesome family and ready to discuss terms?"

"Yes." Harper glared at Lord Maitland. "Do you ever knock?"

"No, and believe me, the Fords don't get any better at keeping out of each other's business. I would prefer my half-sister to have the comfort of a house too."

Amy frowned at him, disapproving of his apparent eavesdropping on her private conversation with Harper about where they would live, but the man smiled serenely.

"You need to work on that scowl, pet. My other sisters do a much better job of trying to stab me with their stares." Lord Maitland winked, and it was then she noticed his eyes were tipped up at the corners like hers.

It was a trait she had not shared with her mother, and she'd always suspected the shape and color of her eyes had come from her father. Seeing proof in Viscount Maitland's face made her a little giddy after having no family to call her own for so long. She wondered what his sisters looked like. Perhaps, if Lord Maitland was correct, she might meet them one day and determine that for herself. "I will do my best."

"Indeed, you must, for we will not be strangers ever again." His smile grew warmer. "Come along, Mr. Cabot. I have found pen and paper enough for a proper contract."

"Is this not a job for her father or a solicitor?"

"Trust me, you do not want Lord Templeton to write a contract that includes your name. Not ever." The viscount scowled fiercely. "I am well versed in the details of contract law to protect my family. It is something of a hobby, although my secretary can probably find every hole a contract could possibly have. I will have you sorted out before my mother can finish compiling her list of potential spouses to introduce you to during the next season."

"She wouldn't do that." Amy gasped, casting a startled glance at Harper.

"How little you know of her true nature," Lord Maitland mused "She has already engaged a dressmaker to visit you tomorrow, a cobbler for the day after, and God knows what else. There is nothing she enjoys more than arranging someone else's life. I snuck out to meet you tonight in case I needed to save you from her plotting to have you married before the month is out. However, since Mr. Cabot's rather thunderous scowl indicates a strong desire to keep with his original plan and wed you himself, we'd best proceed with all due haste."

He strode forward and gallantly held out his arm. "I'm of a mind to attend the wedding too if you've no objection. In fact, I think I must insist upon it."

"I would be honored," Amy choked out. She glanced at Harper quickly. "I hope this hasn't changed your mind."

He took her other arm. "My dear, not in a hundred years."

Amy took another step, but he halted her.

"Wait," Harper said. "I have something to give you."

He dug in his waistcoat pocket and produced the ring she had seen him with that morning. Her stomach lurched at the realization he intended to give her Diana Cabot's wedding ring. "There's no need to give me something so dear to you."

He frowned and held up the ring. "This was my mother's. I received it when she died and put it away. Would you not consider it as your own? My parents had a happy marriage."

"It was not your late wife's?"

"No. She never wore it. Diana preferred the ring I gave her when we wed. She thought wearing two was excessive."

He held the ring up so she could admire it. "I would give you anything you want, Amy. Anything at all."

Amy held out her trembling hand, fingers splayed. He had been thinking of her that morning too, and not just about Diana Cabot. Oh, the dear man. "I should be very pleased to wear your ring, sir."

He slipped the ring onto her finger, and it was a perfect fit. "At last, something of mine you will not argue about taking."

She eased closer to Harper. "I accepted your kisses and your love without question."

"You did indeed." He teased her jaw with his fingers. "I am grateful for you, Amy. You brought me to life again."

Amy kissed him quickly, and kept kissing him until Lord Maitland forced them apart ten minutes later with a threat of sending for Lady Templeton to conduct the negotiations in person.

Suitably chastened, Amy and Harper kept their hands to themselves, at least until Lord Maitland was on his way home.

The End

PREVIEW: AN AFFAIR SO RIGHT

*Heartbroken and desperate, an unmarried lady temporarily enters
the employ of a disastrously disorganized and distracting viscount
in a bid to prove her father's death more than an accident.*

If there was anything in life surer to turn a man's stomach, it was a
blatant attempt at matchmaking over a mahogany dining table.
Quinn Ford, formerly a captain in His Majesty's navy but now
more happily Viscount Maitland, would rather be run through in
battle than be the focus of his father's machinations to see him
miserably wed to the mouse of a woman perched at his side.

"Have you visited Tattersalls yet?" he asked her to be polite.

Miss Genevieve Cushing uttered a negative squeak to his
question and then buried her face in her water glass again.

He sighed in resignation. Miss Cushing was without the
courage to answer anyone with confidence, or even to look his
mother in the eye it seemed. He fell silent and turned his attention
back to his plate.

Quinn had not resumed a public life in society to put up with missish nonsense. He admired forthright women. Prim and proper Miss Cushing, daughter of a wealthy London merchant, a connection most likely indebted to his father in some way, was most certainly not his type of female. She had none of the presence required to be a future Duchess of Rutherford when the title fell to him eventually. Not that he had ever wished ill on his beloved grandsire.

Which was not the case when it came to his own father—Lord Templeton—seated farther down the table from him.

Quinn glanced along to where his father sat holding court. Father was probably destined to live forever.

"You should have your brother take you one day," he said to Miss Cushing.

"He's very busy," she whispered.

George Cushing was probably visiting brothels with his intemperate friends right now. He was young and reckless. But who was Quinn to judge another man's priorities?

He was only concerned about people who affected his own life, and Miss Cushing would never be one of them.

Quinn's future wife would need to be possessed of firm convictions to survive his future, because when Templeton became the Duke of Rutherford, there was no telling what evil would befall him and the gentler members of the family. The family had already suffered due to Templeton's grasping nature.

He considered what other arrangements his father had made with Mr. Cushing besides attending this dinner. Nothing good for the Cushings, most likely. Quinn knew firsthand it was never wise to make any deal with Lord Templeton. People who did tended to be vastly unhappy with the result.

"Gentlemen, if you will excuse us, we will leave you to your simple pleasures," Mama, the Countess Templeton, announced as she set her napkin aside and rose from her chair at the end of the meal.

Quinn was quick to reach his feet, as were the other gentlemen, who protested she was leaving them too soon. His mother was an exceptionally popular woman in London society, hardly meek and most certainly not missish, and still attractive at fifty years of age. Quinn adored her, and so did everyone else. Quinn's mother was respected, whereas his father was feared.

Mother urged the women to go with her, giving way for the gentlemen to partake of port and cigars after dinner. She gave Quinn a brief but pointed look that spoke volumes from her husband's shadow. *Tread carefully* it said.

Quinn inclined his head to her as she moved toward him at a stately pace. He'd grown accustomed to such unspoken warnings from his mother, and where he could, he heeded them all. Thwarting the Earl of Templeton's manipulations had become their life's work.

Her attention strayed to the young woman lingering by his chair, and her eyes narrowed with a hint of displeasure.

Mama had shared her guest list with him yesterday, and at that time, the Cushings had not been included for this remembrance dinner in honor of his late sister. They had not known his sister Mary. The Cushings were new additions; included, most likely, at Lord Templeton's express demand.

Mama grasped Miss Cushing's elbow and led her by subtle force toward the drawing room and away from Quinn. He hid a smile, grateful that when it came to matrimony, he and his mother were of the same mind regarding his future. She wished him to marry for love, so she thwarted her husband at every opportunity.

The other women trailed after Mama, chattering happily and laughing among themselves as they fled into the drawing room for tea and a good gossip.

With them gone, Quinn took a turn about the room to stretch his legs and then headed for the decanters of port set aside for the gentlemen to partake from. He poured himself a drink and downed the lot. Dinners with his father required liquid reinforcement be deployed at all times.

He poured another and slid the bottle back into the spot.

Quinn joined Lord Deacon, who was nursing a brandy glass already at the end of the room. "My apologies for missing your cousin's ball last week," Quinn murmured to him.

Deacon, an earl near his age, was widely regarded as an idiot. Deacon did not excel at manly pursuits except for drinking; he did not seek to distinguish himself in parliament, claiming there were wiser voices to be heard. What Deacon did exceedingly well was friendship. He knew—not assumed, while wringing his hands—that sometimes his friends needed to use him as a shield. That was why, when he was invited to dine by the Earl and Countess Templeton, he could always be counted on to attend if Quinn would be there too.

Deacon smiled, glancing around the room as he did to see who was near. "The usual business?"

"Is there anything else that prevents me seeing my friends but my father's orders?"

"None so far, but I am sure that your future wife might have the ability to sway you one day." Deacon's eyes sparkled with mirth, glancing toward the distant drawing room, where Miss Cushing had vanished. "Did Templeton's latest matrimonial prospect catch your fancy?"

"Hardly," Quinn grumbled. Deacon knew the challenges Quinn faced thanks to his overly ambitious father. "I swear she squeaked."

"Could be amusing in the right setting. At least you could find

Miss Cushing in the dark, should you ever misplace her." Deacon laughed suddenly. "Mary would have set down a plate of cheese for her, had you expressed the slightest interest in marrying the girl."

"She would have, too." Quinn raised his glass with a deep sigh. He missed his little sister, but never more so than today—on the anniversary of when she'd ended her life.

"To Puddleduck," Deacon said, raising his glass, too. Deacon was one of the few friends who knew today's significance to them. Suicides were rarely spoken of in polite circles.

Quinn's sister had been seventeen when she'd drowned herself. Three and Twenty in a few weeks' time. It still shocked him that she was gone. Quinn's nose itched, and he forced a laugh out to fight his sadness. "She adored the name you gave her."

"She was a good sport. But at least Puddleduck is better than the nickname *you* gave her," Deacon scowled. "The Pestilence was hardly a respectful name to give any lady."

Mary had been something of a pest as a child, and calling her *the Pestilence* had stuck until her last year. "She never minded the names."

In hindsight, perhaps the nickname hadn't been the best choice to give to his younger sister. No one had sensed her unhappiness or known her emotions were so fragile. Mary had died so young, for reasons that to this day baffled him. His second younger sister had appeared happy one day, full of plans for the future, her season, marriage, and babies, and yet had waded out into the sea at the family estate fully clothed and drowned—as she must have known she would.

Quinn surveyed the room, his thoughts stuck on that tragic day. The sun had been shining, and he'd had good news to share about his new command and had run out to the cliffs to tell her about it. Discovering Mary face down in the churning sea was a shock Quinn would never forget. He hadn't been able to save her. She'd already been gone too long by the time he'd pulled her from the water.

"She gave as good as she got. What was her nickname for you again?"

"Bumblefoot, on account of my lack of prowess on the dance floor," Deacon said glumly. "At least that was accurate. I still can't dance well enough to please the ladies I like."

Mary had been Deacon's friend. Quinn had assumed they'd marry once Mary came of age, and she finally noticed Deacon had adored the ground she walked on. They had always been whispering to each other and laughing over the silliest things no one else had found remotely funny. Deacon had taken her death as hard as any member of the family.

All except for Father. Templeton hadn't shed a tear.

Quinn regarded his parent as he spoke loudly and with great enthusiasm without any respect for the anniversary they had planned to mark today. Templeton had covered up the suicide swiftly and had told everyone to forget her.

Quinn couldn't do that and had suffered for his disobedience.

Mother openly marked each anniversary just to spite her husband.

"Maitland?" Deacon regarded him solely, and the softly spoken word drew him back from the dark abyss of his grief and anger. It was always there, catching him off guard. He couldn't accept that he'd never know why she'd died.

He forced his fists to uncurl. "Father and Mr. Cushing are as thick as thieves tonight, but I'd rather die without an heir than marry his daughter."

"I'd like a smart wife who was happy to put up with a fool like me." Deacon's grin faded to apprehension. "Watch out. He's got that look about him. Oh, damn and blast it. He's coming our way," Deacon complained

Quinn quickly turned his back on the room to peer out the window. Outside, Londoners were going about their business without a care in the world. And the world was finally at peace. Napoleon was locked up; the French army and navy thwarted by the might of the British forces. Life should be pleasant.

Except that it couldn't be while his father pursued his own agenda to direct Quinn's life.

"Ah, Lord Templeton," Deacon bellowed with great enthusiasm. "Excellent dinner as usual. Your dear wife has outdone herself yet again. My sincere compliments to your cook and staff, too. I can't remember the last time I've ever felt so full, except for Lord Sanderson's dinner last week. But do you know I had to turn down a second helping of that fine pork chop that night because it left the faint aftertaste of lemon in my mouth? None of that at your table here, of course. Lady Templeton would never allow such culinary faux pas beneath your roof, would she?"

Quinn struggled not to grin. Deacon could natter on about dinners, and the food served to him, for hours on end. He bored everyone with his little speeches—always on purpose. It was a useful skill Quinn couldn't hope to emulate but appreciated. Deacon could play the fool at will without breaking a sweat.

"A man can indeed have too much of a good thing," Quinn agreed, bravely joining into the conversation because it would irritate the hell out of his father that he would side with Deacon.

"I require a word with my son, Lord Deacon," Father said abruptly.

"Oh. Oh, yes of course. Certainly. Go right ahead," Deacon offered.

Quinn turned slightly to acknowledge his father, but nearly laughed out loud as it became clear that Deacon wasn't leaving them, and remained planted at Quinn's side with his arms crossed over his wide chest.

Immovable.

Seeming unaware he wasn't wanted.

"In private," Lord Templeton growled, before jerking his head toward the hallway door. "Perhaps you could deliver your compliments to Lady Templeton in person."

"Oh, of course." Deacon smacked his forehead, eyes wide. "I'd best rejoin the ladies then."

With one last happy smile to Father, Deacon rushed away like a hapless schoolboy.

Lord Templeton scowled. "You should end your friendship with that dullard."

"He's a good man," Quinn replied, having suffered the demand many times before.

"Forever nattering on about pork chops and lemon as if I care about such things."

Father couldn't abide idle conversation. He was too impatient to care about anyone but himself.

"Mary liked him," Quinn said with a sincere smile. Mention of Mary was one spectacular way to stop any topic of conversation in its tracks. It worked every time. "She was the one who asked me to include him in my circle of friends, and I promised I would watch out for him."

Father tossed off his head, jaw clenching briefly. "What did you think of her?"

Ah, there it was—the real reason for Templeton's rude interruption. "Of whom?"

"The Cushing chit. Her father owns a thousand acres at Colchester and has no heir apparent. She'll inherit everything I hear." Templeton gestured to the gentleman in question, eyes narrowed and assessing. "She would be a good match for you."

For anyone but Quinn. "Doubtful."

Father looked at him with the dead-eyed stare of a furious man. "It is time you gave up these foolish notions and made an advantageous match."

"I'm not marrying a woman I don't care deeply for."

"That's your mother's new nonsense clouding your head."

Quinn snorted out loud. "You and Mother married as strangers and never became the closest of couples. No wonder she highly recommends love matches over cold alliances like yours."

Father's hand finally twitched at his side as Quinn scored a hit. The topic of his parents' union was a tricky one. His parents barely spent any time together these days and everyone knew it. Father had married Mother for her enormous dowry. He had kept a mistress since Quinn was at least ten years of age.

Templeton's glory days were over though. His hair was more gray than black, and he'd developed a definite paunch these past few years. When angry, his face mottled an unhealthy red, as it did now.

"Do not speak ill of your mother," Templeton warned.

"I would never disparage *Mother*." His mother put up with so much and never complained except for lack of grandchildren to hold in her arms. However, his sister Sally was well on the way to fulfilling that request, thanks to her recent marriage.

Father grabbed his arm. "Impertinent whelp. How dare you."

"I won't allow you to choose my bride for me," Quinn said in a mild tone. "I will make up my own mind about when I marry, too. You may scheme until your face is blue, but when I marry, believe me, it will not be for the good of my purse alone."

The grip on his arm tightened to painful levels. "You will call on Miss Cushing tomorrow," Templeton insisted.

Quinn had borne worse punishments and kept his face impassive. "I will not. I came to dinner tonight to remember Mary, with people who knew and loved her. I've no idea why you would disrespect Mother *or* Mary by forcing strangers upon us at such a time. We loved her more than you ever did."

Father dug his fingers deeper, just as the other gentlemen stood and began to move noisily about the room. Quinn remained still, enduring the pain without flinching or pulling away. He'd been doing so for years. "Do not embarrass Mother, tonight of all nights," Quinn warned.

Templeton released Quinn immediately.

Deacon returned, his face beaming an idiot smile. "Ah, Maitland. Are you free now to complete our conversation?"

"Indeed." Deacon's timing was impeccable. Despite his father's plans, Quinn was determined to make his own way, to live his own life in peace now that the war was over. That was why he'd resigned his command so quickly after the war, before his father could hatch a new scheme designed to keep Quinn in his clutches.

He moved toward his friend without a backward glance for his father's permission. He slapped Deacon on the shoulder and turned him toward the drawing room. "Now, tell me more about this problem you have?"

Deacon winced. "I'm afraid I'm going to need rather a lot of your help."

"For what?"

"Finding a woman for me to marry, of course."

"Oh." Quinn stared at Deacon in astonishment. "I didn't think you were serious about that."

"Well, I am." Deacon protested. "I'm tired of women who just want to sit on my lap a few times and then pretend they didn't fancy me after all."

Quinn choked on an oath. Now there was a picture he'd rather not have in his mind. "Ah, Deacon, now is really not the time for specifics of your intimate relations. When we're done here, we could talk at my home if that suits?"

Deacon nodded quickly. "I knew I could depend on you."

Purchase your copy to keep reading

MORE REGENCY ROMANCE

Distinguished Rogues Series

Chills ~ Broken ~ Charity ~ An Accidental Affair

Keepsake ~ An Improper Proposal ~ Reason to Wed

The Trouble with Love ~ Married by Moonlight

Lord of Sin ~ The Duke's Heart ~ Romancing the Earl

One Enchanted Christmas ~ Desire by Design

His Perfect Bride ~ Pleasures of the Night ~ Silver Bells

Seduced in Secret ~ Yours Until Dawn

Wild Randalls Series

Engaging the Enemy ~ Forsaking the Prize

Guarding the Spoils ~ Hunting the Hero

Saints and Sinners Series

The Duke and I ~ A Gentleman's Vow

An Earl of Her Own ~ The Lady Tamed

Rebel Hearts Series

The Wedding Affair ~ An Affair of Honor

The Christmas Affair ~ An Affair so Right

...and many more

ABOUT HEATHER

USA Today Bestselling Author Heather Boyd believes every character she creates deserves their own happily-ever-after—no matter how much trouble she puts them through. With that goal in mind, she writes steamy romances that skirt the boundaries of propriety to keep readers enthralled until the wee hours of the morning. Heather has published over fifty regency romance novels and shorter works full of daring seductions and distinguished rogues. She lives north of Sydney, Australia, with her trio of rogues and pair of four-legged overlords.

Find out more about Heather at:
Heather-Boyd.com

facebook.com/HeatherBoydRomanceAuthor

instagram.com/heatherboydbooks

bookbub.com/authors/heather-boyd

goodreads.com/Heather_Boyd